I0565819

DESIRING MORE

By the Author

Date Night

Desiring More

Visit us at www.boldstrokesbooks.com

DESIRING MORE

by

Raven Sky

2021

DESIRING MORE

© 2021 By Raven Sky. All Rights Reserved.

ISBN 13: 978-1-63679-037-4

This Trade Paperback Original Is Published By
Bold Strokes Books, Inc.
P.O. Box 249
Valley Falls, NY 12185

First Edition: September 2021

THIS IS A WORK OF FICTION. NAMES, CHARACTERS, PLACES, AND INCIDENTS ARE THE PRODUCT OF THE AUTHOR'S IMAGINATION OR ARE USED FICTITIOUSLY. ANY RESEMBLANCE TO ACTUAL PERSONS, LIVING OR DEAD, BUSINESS ESTABLISHMENTS, EVENTS, OR LOCALES IS ENTIRELY COINCIDENTAL.

THIS BOOK, OR PARTS THEREOF, MAY NOT BE REPRODUCED IN ANY FORM WITHOUT PERMISSION.

CREDITS
Editor: Barbara Ann Wright
Production Design: Stacia Seaman
Cover Design by Tammy Seidick

Acknowledgments

My first thank you for this book goes to Paula. I've never had a lover enter my imaginative world as deeply and fully as you. I suspect my characters are almost as alive for you as they are for me. You provided inspiration, encouragement, critique, and even fan fiction. Thank you for believing in my stories and in me.

Thank you to my partner, Shelley, as well, for listening patiently to each story, and for holding space for me to get lost in creating, while keeping our household running smoothly. Practical support is an underrated gift for creative types. Thank you for all the love and the snacks!

Another big, genuine thank you is owed to the Bold Strokes Books team, for supporting lesbian voices and for making a commitment to amplify racialized voices too. The fraught connection between Emma and Win in "First Contact," as well as the inner turmoil that Sarah struggles with over her mixed-race heritage in "Tough as Nails," are manifestations of my own struggles, as well as the struggles of my home country of Canada, where indigenous people and settlers have a lot of healing and reconciliation to attend to.

In real life, as in these pages, there is always hope. I've written these stories over many years, and this book has given me a precious opportunity to look over the range of my erotic writing and to discover commonalities. One thread that weaves through all of them is the transformational, healing power of sex and love. In my stories, characters struggle. They struggle to find their voice, to find love, to find understanding, to belong. But through interaction with another who is different, they find something that they needed. They leave the connection transformed. Sex can be mundane. But it can also be magical. Most of my stories are about encounters with difference. Someone who is another age, another race, another personality type. Xenophobia, the fear of difference, is the root of so many of our world's problems. But in my stories, I try to highlight how diversity is a source of strength. And sexy as all hell!

I want to dedicate this book to the all the feisty women who refuse to settle. Who desire and seek out more from life. Who follow their hearts and their pussies wherever they should be called. Settling is a bit of a fraught concept for me, because as a writer, I sometimes wonder why I keep writing erotica when I could be writing in more respected genres. But erotica calls to me because I think the world could use more pleasure, more joy. After all, erotica need not be formulaic smut focused purely on body parts coming together. I try to infuse my erotica with literary elements, historical research, spiritual truths, feminist empowerment, and a hearty dash of good humour. I can only hope that I've succeeded and that the stories in this collection will bring multiple forms of pleasure to those who encounter them.

Finally, if you are desiring more, dear reader, may you find what you are seeking.

CONTENTS

PART ONE: FARAWAY AND CLOSE AT HAND
TRAVEL EROTICA

FUCK ME LIKE A CANADIAN

There is a heat to attraction. An energy. You can feel it. Undeniable. This was the last place I expected to feel it. Not least of all because it's illegal here. Is it punishable by death? I strained to remember my online research pre-departure. Morocco. LGBTQ rights. What did Google have to reveal about that? My mind blanked. Because her hands were on my naked flesh, lathering me in a traditional black olive oil soap. Something in her actions was more than indifferent. Something in her eyes, when they happened to catch mine, was not impersonal.

She put a kiis on her hand, a kind of scrubbing glove, and asked me to lie down. I arranged myself on the tile floor, suddenly self-conscious, and she set to work, eradicating days of shower-less mountain trekking and sweaty desert camel riding from my body. It was an odd sensation right on the line between pain and pleasure. I wondered if I should feel embarrassed, but the hammam, the public bath, has no place for modesty.

The bath attendant noticed my tattoo, hesitated in her otherwise practiced motions, and asked, "Is this the sign of your people?" I didn't know what to say. The tattoo shows two interlocking women's symbols in rainbow colors, a throwback to my heady first days of coming out. What could I risk here? But she headed me off, lifting a long and silky mane of hair to show her own surprising tattoo gracing the back of her neck. I recognized the symbol. "Berber," she said. "My people." Berbers are the original people of Morocco, the first inhabitants who lived here before the Arabs came and colonized.

I complimented the design, and she smiled. I tried not to pay attention, to dismiss the electric erotic tension. But this was where it started. This improbable romance between a white tourist and a Berber beauty. Unbelievable.

She complimented my dreads and invited me to a women's party. I knew enough to read between the lines and accepted the invitation with a mix of dread and excitement. This was dangerous. And yet I'd never roamed the planet seeking the comfort of the known. The thrill of travel was about stepping outside of everything I knew and risking misadventure, and so I went to the party. All women. All gay, from what I could glean. A secret underworld of sisters who looked out for one another. I was enthralled.

We fucked for the first time there, Till and I. After a few hours spent drinking wine and singing incomprehensible Berber songs, occasionally dancing with ludicrous abandon, she pulled me into a private room and shut the door meaningfully. The music was turned up outside, and though I spoke another language, I read the signs correctly. She was flushed from dancing, pink-cheeked, eyes afire, and I felt nervous, unsure what was expected in this new context. But I didn't have to do anything. She was intentional. Stripped for me knowingly, a mocking smile teasing the corners of her mouth. And I just stood there, mesmerized and drunkenly stupefied by the sight of all that undulating tan flesh so enticingly within reach.

Her breasts were full and weighty, her stomach achingly round, hips perfect curves. I was overcome. Do I make a move now? I wondered, questioning my role in this foreign interaction, but she left little room for such questions, her fingers working deftly to rid me of my clothing, the last barrier between us.

That night was nothing less than torturous. Till loved every inch of my exterior, caressing, licking, biting, lightly scratching every morsel of my flesh but never entering me. Always careful. I remembered things I'd read in a biography about a Western trekker working his way across the Sahara, encountering intimate cultural confusion with Moroccan women along the way until he learned the unwritten rule that you could play, but you could not penetrate, for that was the prerogative of future husbands. And so he learned to "paint," a not uncommon Middle Eastern form of foreplay, in which a man uses the tip of his penis like a paintbrush to create elaborate patterns upon the beloved's vulva.

I remembered this through clenched jaw and thrusting hips as Till used the tip of her breast to tantalize me. Her nipples slowly tracing the shape of my lips, spreading wetness into intricate patterns, lulling, maddening, intoxicating, un-fucking-bearable. So close. So fucking enraging. I teetered on the precipice of climax until tears sprang to my eyes with the frustration of knowing that it would never happen, not without the hot rush of her fingers inside me. Was it wrong to ask? Was it unthinkable here?

Her fingers took over for her ample breast, continuing the maddening artwork, and my whole body trembled on the edge. I couldn't care. I grabbed her by the back of her hair to pull her close and half whispered, half growled, "I want you inside me...please."

Her rhythm halted, her face registered surprise, and then a small smile upturned her cheeks, and she was inside me. Warmth flooded me, concentrated where she moved within me, and within a few short minutes, I was coming loudly as she was laughing and trying to shush me while the music outside increased rather thoughtfully in volume.

That was how we started, Till and me.

What a whirlwind we were. Reckless. Giddy with lust. What she saw in me I was never sure about. Was I just a story she would impress the local closet dykes with? A story about her silly fling with a weird-haired foreigner, a white girl she'd managed to seduce? Mind you, was that how I would speak of her, albeit in reverse? Would I similarly reduce this to some tale of an alien dalliance with a mysterious woman from a faraway land? Who here was fetishizing the other, and what was the pure curiosity of inexplicable natural attraction? I couldn't say. I just knew that I was enthralled with her, and it *was* wrapped up in the differences she embodied.

I traveled a lot, hostel hopping from country to country, and so I knew the sweet intensity of a vacation romance was partially about its inherently time-limited nature. This could not last, and we both knew it. One morning, waking in my tiny hostel room, she asked me about my plans. I told her I had another week in Morocco, and Essaouira was next on my hope-to-see list.

She avoided my eyes, and fiddling with one of my dreads, she mentioned she could take time off from the hammam, that her boss, whose home we had partied at that first night, would understand. She was painfully beautiful in that moment, vulnerable, desirous. I toyed with pushing her boundaries.

Watching her face carefully, I teased, "Only if you finally let me fuck you." This had been a struggle from the beginning. Till was generously attentive but always refused to let me return the attention.

Many feelings crossed her face in rapid succession, but she settled on joy. "Before you leave," she promised and snuggled into me.

And so we said good-bye to bustling Marrakesh with its scammy snake charmers, transvestite belly dancers, and aggressive street hustlers. We said hello to the seaside, to gulls and open-air cafés and hippie wanderers. We knew our time together was ending, but that just concentrated everything. My second to last night, we sat in a seaside bar by the beach and watched boys playing soccer in the sand. We ordered beers. The waiter brought them but frowned at Till, disapproving.

She looked him right in the eye and chugged. I laughed. "Do you know what my name means?" Till inquired. I shook my head. "It's Tilleli. In Berber, that means freedom." She laughed. "My mother should have named me more carefully."

I asked about her family, but her eyes went hard, and she just drank her beer, so I stared out at the water and wondered about this woman I barely knew. About how in a few days, I would be back in Canada where I could be the lesbiannest lesbian who ever lesbianed, and nobody would care, and she'd still be here, hiding, risking her freedom with every encounter.

"Do you ever think of leaving?" I asked after a pause.

"This is my life," she said simply.

I pushed. "Yeah, but you could go somewhere else, somewhere where you could be freer," I insisted.

She turned slowly to look at me, the hardness still in her eyes, and said absolutely nothing. She turned back to the water. I'd said something stupid, but I didn't know why or what. What did I not understand? I couldn't know.

The last night, we fought. There were tears and apologies, and "I just don't want you to go." The usual, typical, doomed-romance girl-drama. But it was potent. Emotional tension shifts so easily to sexual tension, and she fucked me furiously up against the wall of our little room, fucked me like there was no tomorrow, because there wasn't. Not for us. And when we were done and exhausted, a crumpled sweaty heap on the floor, I saw she was crying.

I never know what to do when women cry. I went to wipe her tears away, but she grabbed my hand and held it tightly, looked me in the eyes intently, and said, "I want you to fuck me like a Canadian." I started to laugh because it was so incongruous, this sudden ludicrous image I had of fucking her up against a snowman. She was wearing only a toque, and I was licking maple syrup from her naked, shivering flesh as a friendly moose ambled by. It was stupid and inexplicable, and I could see I was offending her, but I couldn't stop laughing.

She threw on clothes and made to leave. I hurried to stop her, but she was out the door. I dressed hastily and ran after her. She'd gone to the courtyard. It was after midnight, and the air was cool. I could see the night sky just bursting with stars from here. I tried to explain. "I'm sorry. I just don't know what you mean by 'like a Canadian.' It confused me, and I laughed. I'm sorry." It was a long, drawn-out affair, but eventually, I won her back over and figured out what she meant. She wanted penetration, unusual for non-married women who play here. "Are you sure?"

"It's not like you'd be the first. Don't be so full of yourself." Great. Because insults and anger were the way to set the mood. But I knew it was just about me leaving, and so I moved in to make this work.

I grabbed her face in both hands and forced her to look at me, to stop, to feel the way our breasts were pressed up against one another. I didn't say anything, just waited for her eyes to soften, and when I knew she felt it, then I kissed her. Slow, sweet, holding back, a shy first sort of kiss. I felt her shiver. We both smiled. I kissed her again, savoring her taste, the warmth of her breath mingling with mine. Her arms were around my waist, and my tongue began to dance with hers, so slow, so sweet. I went to lift her shirt. She raised her arms, inviting, and I watched as the fabric rolled across her torso and full breasts, over her head and down to the floor. I brought my mouth close to hers, and it opened expectantly, but I didn't kiss her mouth, I brought my lips to her jawline, her neck, her shoulders, her breasts. I lingered here. Cupped the swell of her in my hands and teased her nipples for a time. She shifted her weight and made small noises of pleasure. My hands slipped beneath the waist of her skirt, and I pulled it down the length of her legs.

In her hasty dressing, there was no time for underthings, and she was magnificently naked.

I looked around for an appropriate space. There was a stray towel by an intricately tiled fountain, and I laid it down with extravagant care, smoothing all the corners and acting ridiculously like it was a bed fit for a queen. We both smiled, and she approached, kneeled on the towel, and tried to unbutton me, but I demurred, just as she had done many times before. This was all her. She lay down, her eyes twinkling with a faint hint of daring, her knees up and locked together. I like to remember her right there. In that moment. In a courtyard in Essaouira. Surrounded by snoring tourists. Just waiting for me to fuck her silly. Looking so utterly tempting in the moonlight. In my memories, I linger here.

In reality, I didn't. I went to town. I'd been waiting so long to touch her that eager would be an understatement. I held her eyes, met their daring, and opened her legs. I feasted on her like a man dying of thirst in the desert feasts at an oasis. I wish I could say I was more suave, more controlled, but I was drunk with delight and abandon. She came before I entered her. So we dallied before take two, losing ourselves in bottomless kisses.

I was deliriously tired. That might have contributed to the random, uninvited images that kept popping into my head as we built up to another go. "Fuck me like a Canadian." It was still funny. This time we were on a frozen pond, hockey players skating all around us, politely averting their eyes as I used my mouth to roll up her rim…oh yeah! *That's stupid, stop thinking about that.*

I focused on the task at hand. I had primed her clit sufficiently now. She was slick with desire, and now was the time to give her what she wanted. I slipped a finger inside her gingerly. She was tight, but her whole body reacted, and I knew it was good. I worked away, patiently, focused, listening intently to her reactions and adjusting my pace and fingers accordingly. Her breath was speeding up. Her hips were encouraging a particular rhythm. I kept at it. Now she was peaking, now we were getting there, her hips became more insistent, her sounds more unthinking. But it was a long freaking climb to her summit. My arms began to ache, my fingers to cramp, but I kept on trekking. She was flooding now. I could feel her wetness splashing up my arm, almost to my elbow. I held in there. I kept the beat. I didn't miss a step because I was Canadian, goddammit, and we were dependable little beavers. The Mountie always got his man. My country was counting on me. She wanted to be fucked like a Canadian, eh? The glory of the maple leaf depended right now on my ability to keep this pumping steady, adding just the right twist at just the right moment.

I imagined myself at the UN headquarters with Justin Trudeau with his McDreamy hair and feminist principles presenting me with a special award for international diplomacy. It came with a lifetime supply of Tim-bits and bragging rights as Chief Canuck Pussy Whisperer. k.d. lang would be pissed. Ha, I out-dyked you, I gloated inside my head as singing filled the air. Wait, that was real. There was singing. What the fuck?

I looked down at Till, and at just that moment, her pussy erupted, her muscles clenched and shot out my hand as her body spasmed, and her scream joined the singing. I was so confused. Was I that exhausted? My arms felt like floppy spaghetti, but was my mind similarly cooked? I fell down beside Till on the sopping wet towel, shaking all over. That was when I realized it was the call to prayer. The singing. It was the mosque, calling worshippers to the first early morning prayer. So my mind was only half-baked. It all made sense.

I love the memory of that ridiculous, gorgeous night like I love that sound. And now when I hear it, I think of Till, this beautiful, fierce, brave woman I once had a short time to love. Wherever I am, when I hear the call of the sacred, I think of her.

THE LAY OF THE LAND

I am ear deep in pussy. I mean, *ear deep* in pussy. Like, *I can feel her wetness trickling behind my ears and into my hair, and now it's going to go curly, and I wasted twenty minutes straightening my hair for this date, but now when we're done, I'm going to look ridiculous,* ear deep in pussy. And I'm in that space of going down when it's almost trance-like. Just me and the pussy. Just me and this rhythm. Just me and this texture. Me and this moving moisture as I create abstract art with my tongue, and everything is stripped down to essence. Pure form. Not that this woman whose pussy I am currently ear deep in doesn't matter. She does. This offering most intimate is precious, I know. I know that knowing her this way—her taste, breath, movements—is a kind of sacred. But in this moment, I am blissfully lost to anything but this quintessence of what it means to be a woman and a dyke.

❖

I had the best sex of my life in Thailand. I was twenty-four and had come with a bunch of friends to celebrate finishing university. It was one of those notorious full-moon parties on the beach. So many details of that night are still so vivid. Sipping god-awful Thai whiskey out of a little sandcastle bucket. My feet shuffling in the sand to the sound of pulsating beats fighting to be heard over the roar of the waves and the wind off the sea. The feeling of elation and achievement for being the first in my family to graduate.

I remember the moment I saw her. There was a troupe of fire dancers performing. All young Thai guys aged thirteen to twenty-five, most likely. They were amazing. But they also scared me with their seemingly reckless bravado, juggling flame, creating ever more daring stunts and pieces of pyrotechnic performance art. They were throwing a flaming baton to each other across the makeshift dance floor set up in the sand, and with something about the way her arm raised, I could see the tiny but unmistakable swell of her breasts, and it was like an instant rush of heat as I looked closer to scrutinize her face, her throat, her hands, her hips to confirm her femaleness. Despite her close-cropped hair and boyish clothes, she was definitely a woman. Hanging out with guys and literally playing with fire.

I was hooked. I couldn't stop staring. And she must have noticed because when she needed a volunteer for her act, she came right to me. Offered me her hand and a crooked smile. With my friends hooting loud encouragement, I walked onstage, ready to do just about anything she asked. She gestured for me to sit in a chair and mimed over the music for me to put a cigarette in my mouth. I was a smoker then, which I find really hard to believe now, but it was much more common then, and I was twenty-four and stupid. What can I say?

She came close to my face and yelled in my ear, "Don't move. Just breathe." Then she lit two flaming balls and danced them all around me dramatically before making them whirl in a fast-spinning circle in front of my face right before the cigarette. I got that I was supposed to light the thing, but I was so scared I could barely breathe, despite her instructions. I was sure my hair was going to catch on fire any second. I managed to light it, though, and the crowd erupted in laughter and applause. She stepped back and made eye contact with me. Kind of smirking. Amused. I took the cigarette out of my mouth and laughed. I didn't know what else to do.

Then the music changed, and they brought out a limbo pole all lit up in fiery red Christmas lights, and I lost her in the shuffle of the crowd. My friends all jostled to my side, carrying on about how cool that was, so I turned my attention back to my gang and our quest to make epic party memories. I drank more. I danced more. I watched the sky in awe as a dry lightning storm lit up the horizon over the Andaman Sea, but no rain fell. It was magic. Powerful. All the elements in play: wind, water, fire, earth. I felt incredibly alive.

That was when she grabbed my hand. The fire dancing was over, and the dance floor had long been reclaimed by partiers, so I was surprised to see her. She led me away past the DJ to a closed side stall of sorts. She sort of pushed me against it, then stood back and looked at me strangely. She stepped closer, put her hand on my waist and said, "Yes?" with a rising inflection.

Those were the only words she ever said to me: "Don't move. Just breathe." And "Yes?" Because after I nodded, there were no words. Just her hands moving confidently on my body, the left cradling the back of my head as she kissed me, the right grabbing my ass beneath my skirt.

I've returned to that moment so many times in my mind that I could tell you every little thing that she did in order. But it wasn't really about that. It was about that moment. In my life. In that place. With this stranger whose name I never learned. It was how receptive I felt to what life had to offer. How open and trusting and adventurous I felt to pleasure. Well, that's what I think now at forty-one, but probably at twenty-four, it really was just how fucking talented she was with her fingers and mouth. She knew what she was doing, and though I knew I was proving true every stereotype about slutty foreigners, I came hard and loud in the protection of her arms, under a distant purple sky, lit up with lightning.

So it's really not so surprising that I returned here, so many years, so many heartbreaks afterward. Well, one particularly difficult heartbreak afterward. I fled here in a perfectly banal middle-age crisis, I suppose. Just up and left. Didn't tell my family or friends, and signed a two-year contract to teach overseas. It was cruel, but it felt necessary. A viciously abrupt break. Like Sandrine did it. Just walking out after seven years with little more than a "This isn't working for me anymore" as explanation.

I'd moped around, floundering for a time, but once I bought the plane ticket, somehow, I could breathe better. I had a plan. However irrational. But it was only irrational superficially. I had given up so many pieces of myself over the years to make Sandrine happy. I hadn't even noticed. Didn't even mind. Now I wanted to remember who I was, and when I thought about my life and where I had felt most free, most pulsating with youth and certainty of who I was and what I could be, it was here. So here's where I found myself again.

Except this time, I was not celebrating achievement. I was mourning failure. I wasn't young, carefree, and confident. I was middle-aged, stressed out, and uncertain. Which is probably how I got myself into this awkward situation. It was laughable. Pathetic really. How could I possibly be so stupid as to wind up in bed with someone half my age having truly awful sex?

She was so obviously flirting, and it confused me, but it also felt good to be wanted. And maybe that was what I needed. Maybe I was like an old car battery that needed a boost of youthful energy. So I invited her home with me.

And now I am naked and regretting it and trying to speed things along without faking an orgasm because I refuse that on principle. It's a personal rule that you've got to earn it. And she will never earn it with her tiny hands and strangely robotic movement: moving her fingers all the way in and then all the way out, all the way in and then all the way out, like they're on an automated timer for a Fuckomatic Z10.

Yes, this is what I'm thinking about as she fucks me. She asks, "You like?"

I dodge the question, saying, "I think you're very sexy." Great. Now I'm diverting her attention from the problem like she's a freaking toddler. I'm having sex with an incompetent robot toddler. I'm drying up like a desert here, and it's about to get even more awkward. I have to do something.

I tried giving some direction earlier, and that was not well-received. I tried to touch my clit, and that was also shut down. "I know what you like," she said. Great, I thought, I'm having sex with a bossy, incompetent, robot toddler.

I need to make this work. Save face for both of us. I need sexy thoughts. I start to flip through my mental masturbation book. Lesbian nuns? No. Dirty dyke mechanics? No. Ruby Rose on a motorcycle? Overdone.

It's time to pull out the big guns. The Olivia cruise orgy fantasy. Oh yeah. Never fails. Here we go. I'm on the sundeck by the pool. My random imaginary girlfriend is with me. We're topless. Women are making out and making love all over the place. It's a delicious dyke-o-rama on the open seas. All kinds of women. All ages, races, different kinds of beauty, everywhere you look. My girlfriend is holding me from behind as we watch. She plays with my tits. She whispers in my ear, "You like watching all these women fucking?"

"Yes."

"You want me to fuck you too?"

"Yes."

Okay, now we're getting somewhere. I can feel my pussy becoming slick again. But can I come this way? I return to the well-worn fantasy. "You want them to fuck you too?"

"Yes." This usually does the trick. Because in my real life, besides a few youthful indiscretions, I am not particularly sexually adventurous. I've always been in long-term, monogamous relationships, and I haven't been with very many women. So in this fantasy, when my girlfriend holds me from behind, whispering in my ear while other women put their hands on me, it's thrilling, risk-free, fantasy fun. No consequences. Just excess. She's there, strong and firm about what they can and cannot do to me. And I can be as greedy as I want. And I want to fuck them all. Every dyke beautiful in her own way with her scars and her courage and her stories and her unique sexiness. In this fantasy, I offer myself to all of them because it's not real but really hot.

What isn't hot is how my current real-life lover is now slurping on my pussy. And I don't mean metaphorically. She is literally making slurping noises, which I know signifies that something is tasty in Asia, but I still can't handle the sound. Dammit. I was getting somewhere too. Maybe I should just break my rule this once, throw out some *When Harry Met Sally* style shrieks and be done with it. But if I can ignore the slurping sound, it does actually feel good what she's doing with her mouth. I could work with that. So just finish. Just finish the fantasy.

So I do. Enter the captain. In big bold letters. The captain of the Olivia cruise vessel. Top dyke. It's my fantasy so it can be as ridiculous as I like, and it is. She's wearing sailor pants and no shirt. Her tits are tiny and firm. Her arms are awesomely tattooed and absolutely ripped with taut muscles. Her hair is graying and close-cropped. She's tanned. She's muscular. She's power embodied. And she walks the decks of her ship with her arms behind her back, observing. Occasionally barking out orders, or more rarely, doling out praise for a particularly impressive move, position, or orgasm, for those lucky enough to sail on her ship. She watches me. Watches other women's hands on me. And that's always when I come. I can never even get to a point where she fucks me. She just watches me. And our eye contact. The heat between us. Her physical proximity. The possibility. Her body. It puts me over the edge every time, and today is no exception. I finally come, happy to be finished, and push Kanya away from me.

Kanya looks at me expectantly. Expecting what, I'm not sure. And I feel ashamed of my judgment and selfishness. She's young. She's made herself vulnerable. And she's beautiful. Truly a handsome, strapping young baby dyke, or tom as they call them here, short for tomboy. I look at her and feel desire rise inside me. I want to please her. So I do. Going ear-deep in pussy as I described it earlier. And it's transporting and transforming. In ways I didn't expect. It feels invigorating to be knowledgeable and capable of providing so much pleasure this way. It's like…it's like finding my own power again, and as she comes over and over on my face, on my hands, with messy exuberant passion. It's like remembering things I forgot, things I used to be: strong, free, confident, full of possibility. Deeply alive.

I had the best and the worst—and the most transformational—sex of my life in Thailand.

The Arrangement

No fucks given.

If I had to describe what drew me to Dylan in just a few, pithy words, this was what I was too well-bred to say aloud: Dylan didn't give a fuck. But when you grew up like I did, in a *good* family, with *great* business connections, attending the *best* private schools, you were taught to give a fuck about literally everything.

I was sick of it. Sick of listening to the other bored trophy wives bitch about their husbands. Sick of planning charity events that were really just an excuse to show off. Tired of caring what everyone thought of my shoes or my handbag and whether they were quite right. It was exhausting. My life exhausted me, which depressed me because I knew I wasn't really doing anything that merited such exhaustion. My kids were all successfully ensconced in the same prestigious boarding school I'd attended, and though I'd once thought about getting into business for myself, my headstrong father had talked me out of it. He considered it vulgar and an affront to his own ego for his only daughter to dirty her hands with labor. Hadn't he provided eminently, precisely so that I need not worry myself with such things? Thus, resigned to my fate, I mostly busied myself being the face of my father's philanthropic whims when I wasn't busy obsessing over house renovations and assisting the PTA.

I'd met Dylan while preparing to host the middle school welcome party. It was a big to-do. Each year, one family was selected to host the welcome party for each grade, and it was always an elaborate affair, ostensibly a chance for the new students and parents to be welcomed to the school but also, of course, a prime opportunity to gossip and judge. Everything had to be perfect. I'd arranged the usual: renting a tent for the yard, musicians, caterers, decorators, the works, but felt I needed something unique to stand out, a showpiece for the other mothers to envy. Our gardener, Phillip, recommended a living plant sculpture of the school mascot. He said his cousin was really talented at making them, and he showed me some pictures of his cousin's work on his phone. I was impressed and agreed right away.

Dylan was not what I expected. Dylan looked like a teenage boy but was neither a teenager nor a boy. Nor a girl, it seemed. When I awkwardly attempted to ask questions about his cousin, Phillip clued me in.

"Dylan's genderqueer, if that's what you're getting at."

When I stared blankly back at him, he elaborated. "Like not male or female. They used to go by another name, but now they go by Dylan. And you say 'they' or 'them' when you talk about them. Feels kind of weird at first, but you get used to it."

I nodded politely like I understood but felt foolishly lost until further googling helped clarify his meaning. I wasn't completely naive. I had gay friends, and there was a transgender student in my eldest daughter's class, but it was hard to keep up with the terminology and all that it meant. I'd never heard the term "genderqueer" before, but I liked what it meant if it meant the way that Dylan wore their gender as they deftly clipped chicken wire and fashioned it into a pouncing tiger's shape in the late summer sunshine. They sang along to the radio un-self-consciously while stuffing the wire sculpture with moss, then planting chrysanthemums and some dark plant I didn't recognize into alternating black and orange stripes.

The piece was a hit, the talk of the party, and I found excuses to keep Dylan around after that, finding odd jobs for them.

They didn't seem to mind. In fact, they began suggesting odd jobs they could do to help me out around the house too. Their interest seemed more than financial, which alarmed me at first even as it was flattering. I was twice their age. What could they possibly see that was desirable in this boring, middle-aged housewife? But the funny thing was that I didn't *feel* like a boring, middle-aged housewife around Dylan. I felt this strange, electric, long-forgotten spark of something really alive still in me. They liked my stories. They laughed at my jokes. They wanted to know about me. And I wanted to know about them.

And then somehow, we were in Mexico. Alone. Just the two of us. Far from anyone we knew. I thought of it as an "arrangement." Dylan had never traveled, and I was tired of traveling alone. I wanted a companion. We agreed that I would pay, and Dylan would take care of my needs, bringing me drinks, carrying the luggage, applying my sunscreen, keeping me entertained. Whatever I wanted.

That was all. That was what I told myself as I watched them walk back from the bar, balancing two margaritas, making their way toward our lounge sunbed. Damn, they were gorgeous. The bikini top had surprised me, but mixed with men's bathing trunks, it was a perfect blend of masculine and feminine, just like Dylan themself. I couldn't stop myself from staring at the toned, taut expanse of their stomach and the small, firm curve of their chest. Dylan inhabited their body with ease and exuded a kind of simple sensuality in all their movements. I liked watching them.

"M'lady," they cooed, offering up the drink, then jumping onto the sunbed with contented abandon once I'd taken it.

"This place is out of this world," Dylan said, and I tried to see it from their perspective, the perspective of someone who had never traveled. It was undeniably beautiful. Elegant. Elite.

But it was nothing special to me. My father owned a chain of such resorts. In some perverse impulse, I'd booked us at his rival's. Maybe to add to the thrill of tiptoeing to the edge of doing something truly bad for once. Something scandalous. I wrestled with my doubts once more as Dylan bopped to the music wafting over the pool from hidden speakers.

Firstly, there was my husband. If you could call him that. We'd been estranged a long time now but stayed together for appearances. Maybe more. I *did* love him; he was the father of my children. But he had a mistress in New York. He'd wanted to move to New York, where he did a lot of business, and I'd refused, which was when we'd started to grow apart, as his work, and perhaps his heart, kept him there most of the time. He was only ever home a few times a month.

Secondly, there was Dylan themself. Was I being some kind of creepy sugar mama cougar, exploiting my financial power for something shady? I'd hinted at such reservations with Dylan when we first started planning this trip, but they responded with a swift reversal of logic, suggesting that maybe I was the one being taken advantage of. And it did give me pause to consider how it could also be perceived that way, as them preying on the insecure, lonely, older woman, bilking her out of money with their flirty charms.

Dylan interrupted my worries. "Okay, play along with me. Out of all the people around the pool, which one would you choose as a lover?" When I hesitated, they threw in, "Besides me, of course," and actually winked, which made me laugh.

I reluctantly withdrew my eyes from Dylan's twinkling gaze and looked around thoughtfully. Before Dylan, I'd really only ever considered men, but now I found myself scrutinizing everyone carefully. I pointed to a raven-haired beauty with an elaborate tattoo all down her back.

"Why her?"

I pondered. "She seems wild and brave. I want to know what that feels like. What about you?" I was anxious to hear their answer, still uncertain of the authenticity of their attraction to me. Dylan pointed to a blond woman who was loudly dictating very exact orders to a server. Before I could ask why, Dylan offered, "She seems like a bossy bitch who knows what she wants. I like being bossed around by a beautiful woman." Dylan smiled wolfishly, holding my gaze meaningfully until I blushed and looked away.

That night, we dressed up and watched the evening performance together. Dylan looked adorable in a black button-up and sharp gray pants. I realized I'd never seen them dressed up before. In fact, Dylan was usually a little dirty, slightly unkempt, but in the appealingly earthy way of someone who works with their hands. They cleaned up good, as the saying went. And they must have liked my outfit too, for they made me twirl for them and made an approving sound in their throat while I did so.

The dancers were incredible. They sported folk costumes from the Veracruz region. The men wore white pantsuits, complete with white shoes and hats, then a little red scarf. The women had white lace dresses with flouncy skirts and a ruffle at the shoulder. They both seemed to embody the best of the interplay between masculinity and femininity. The women moved gracefully, in flowing circles, with lit votive candles on their heads, the flame dancing alongside them. The men followed, chivalrous in their attentions, their hands held behind their backs. They doffed their hats and tap-danced for the ladies, following their twirling motions. It was mesmerizing. My eyes never left the stage, even as I was very much thrillingly aware that Dylan's thigh was touching mine on the cozy little love seat throughout the entire performance.

Eventually, the performance came to a close, to much enthusiastic applause, as a scarlet ribbon wrapped around the main male dancer was slowly unwound and used to entwine the lead female dancer. She danced her way out of his snare, and the ribbon fell to the ground. They both danced around it for a time before finally revealing that they had used their feet to tie it into a giant bow, presumably symbolizing their union. Dylan and I both added our admiring applause to the crowd's.

We were several drinks in, later that night when Dylan decided they wanted to buy a hat like the one the male dancers had worn. We wandered into the little resort store and looked around, but they only had typical tourist fare. Dylan slapped on a ridiculously oversized sombrero.

"What do you think?"

"I think it will hurt your neck after five minutes. Get a smaller one if you really want one."

"Duly noted. M'lady prefers stamina over size."

I blushed, but the saleslady didn't seem to notice. Dylan pestered me into trying on a flouncy dress like the ones the dancers had worn.

"Come on. We'll play dress-up. It'll be fun. Live a little," they teased.

I reluctantly went into the change-room and tried on the dress.

"What's that? You need help?" Dylan said too loudly before tearing open the curtain that enclosed the little room.

Luckily, I was fully dressed, clutching the red waist ribbon.

"I'm here to serve, right?" Dylan purred. They took the ribbon and moved behind me, wrapping it about my waist with gentle focus. I could feel their breath on my neck, sending shivers down my spine. Their body pressed against mine ever so slightly. We looked at each other in the mirror, transfixed. They pulled the ends of the ribbon slightly, forcing me to lean into them. I closed my eyes and felt a surge of warmth run through me.

Suddenly, the saleslady rushed over, alarmed, and offered help, breaking the spell of the moment.

I tried to pay for the hat, but Dylan wouldn't let me. We decided to have another drink by the beach and started walking that way when Dylan stopped abruptly. "You never look at price tags. Do you know that?"

I stopped too. "I do. Just not in places like that. Honestly, I could have put the inventory of the entire store on my credit card," I confessed. "Does that bother you?"

Dylan considered. "No. It's just like nothing I've ever known before. It's weirdly exciting, actually. You can do and have and be anything you want."

I made a dismissive sound but didn't bother to disillusion them. From their point of view, I knew it was true. But from mine, it wasn't that simple.

Dylan grabbed a tealight from one of the little tables arranged around the pool. They placed it carefully atop the sombrero and started imitating the dancers from earlier this evening. It was stupidly adorable. A passing employee clapped and yelled out something unintelligible in Spanish as he rushed by. Dylan didn't speak Spanish, but that didn't stop them from yelling back random Spanish words nonetheless. "Tortilla. Burrito. Salsa." The tealight tumbled, but Dylan managed to catch it before it smashed on the ground.

"Shit!" They fumbled with the glass, spilling hot wax all over their hand. I rushed to help.

"You're lucky you didn't set your head on fire," I said, turning their hand over to inspect the damage. Luckily, it was only mildly red and irritated.

"A mere flesh wound," they replied, grinning rakishly. Dylan's dark brown eyes held mine with warmth. And something more. A look it took me a moment to recognize as desire; it had been so long since anyone had looked at me like that. I realized how close our faces were. And that I hadn't let go of their hand. I dropped it ungraciously and stepped back, embarrassed.

I could feel Dylan's eyes on me with what seemed to be a mix of amusement and curiosity. My heart was beating wildly, and my thoughts felt all mixed up. It was ridiculous to feel this way. I wasn't a teenage girl anymore. I *had* a teenage girl. I struggled to compose myself.

"Let's go for a dip,' Dylan said.

"I don't know. I don't really want to go all the way back to the room to change."

"Who needs a bathing suit?" Dylan asked, beginning to empty their pockets.

I started to panic. There was free-spirited, and then there was going too far.

Dylan kicked off their shoes. "Don't make me do this alone. You know you want to do something crazy. Let's be crazy! We'll just walk right in." They grabbed my hands and started pulling me toward the stairs that led into the pool.

"Dylan, you're insane. Stop."

"As you wish," they replied, letting go of my hands but continuing to walk backward into the pool. They were submerged to the waist in their fancy clothes, still holding out their arms to me, and it struck me as ridiculously funny and inviting.

Why not be crazy? My father wasn't here to gruffly demand, "Explain yourself," his go-to catchphrase anytime I strayed from the path of being the perfect daughter. My husband was no doubt snuggled up in his mistress's bed. My children were safe. I was free to be and do and have whatever I wanted, right? Wasn't that how Dylan put it?

I looked around. The pool was deserted, lit up, green and turquoise under a star-filled foreign sky. I breathed deeply, then bent to remove my heels, never breaking eye contact with Dylan, who hooted keen approval. It was ridiculous. I was being ridiculous. I could hear my father's disapproving voice in my head. I could imagine the headlines: *Socialite Millionaire's Daughter Caught in Tawdry Queer Sex Scandal at Business Adversary's Resort.* So many levels of betrayal. But I let them fall away, like my inhibitions, as I walked toward

Dylan's eager, outstretched arms. They pulled me close, and we fell into the pool together, laughing with abandon.

"I didn't think you'd actually do it," Dylan managed between bouts of laughter.

"Sometimes I'm braver than I look," I said simply, bringing my body close to theirs, intentionally bridging the distance.

They read the signs accurately and looked around. There was a little bridge over the pool, and Dylan pulled me underneath it, positioning me with my back against the pool's edge, moving in close. We looked at one another for a time, hesitant, as the longing and tension built between us.

"Do you really want to be here?" I said, surprised at my own words. "I mean…with me? Because you don't owe me anything."

"*I want to be here*," Dylan said, enunciating each word carefully and pressing their body into mine. They brought their mouth close my ear. My heart clamored away, unruly in my chest, as they whispered, "What do *you* want? You brought me all the way here to keep you company. So what will it be? How can I please you?"

What did I want? The question flooded me with despair and desire all at once. My body screamed out to be touched, but it was more than any particular act that I wanted. I had no idea what sex would even look like with someone like Dylan. More than anything, I wanted a feeling. Of being seen and wanted and enjoyed for exactly who I was. To feel free to be fully myself. To feel alive again. Desirable and powerful. The way I saw Dylan. But what did Dylan see in me? Why were they here with me when they could be with someone their own age? Someone young, and fresh, and…*nubile*.

I squeaked out the question of why they wanted to be here, and Dylan broke away. "You have a really distorted image of yourself. You know that, right? Yeah, I could be with someone my own age, but why would I be when I could be with someone who's older and more sophisticated and can actually teach me things and take me places like this? You're smart and accomplished and sexy as hell." Dylan was leaning against the far side of the pool's edge now at the other end of the bridge. They looked incredulous but not uncompassionate as they said, "Your life is so full of possibility, and you don't even see it. You're totally free. People would give *anything* for that. It's intoxicating to be so close to that much power."

"I am *not* powerful."

"You *are* powerful," they replied. "You just haven't owned it."

I considered that, letting its import sink in.

"If I took you right here, under this bridge, and we were caught by some random employee, you could probably buy this whole place and hush the whole thing up, couldn't you?"

I smiled at the image of being taken under this very bridge. "Yes, I suppose so."

"*Then you can do anything you want,*" Dylan said, enunciating their words again, like they were willing me to understand something I was missing. They began to cross the space between us. "So...you beautiful, classy, smart woman... *what do you want?*"

I watched the water reflections play off the handsome features of their face and answered without thinking, "Right now, I want you to kiss me."

They didn't hesitate.

They were there to serve, after all.

And what a kiss it was. Breathless, hungry, thrilling. Their hands explored my contours as mine did theirs, and we were oblivious, caught up, utterly enraptured in discovering each other's flesh, until a loud but uncertain voice asked in Spanish if everything was okay.

I rushed to answer that everything was fine in impeccable Spanish, both amused and mortified that Dylan's hypothetical employee had indeed caught us, albeit in a much less compromising interaction than the one they had envisioned.

The employee seemed satisfied, and turned to leave but not before Dylan threw out more of their random Spanish words in ostensible reply: "Nachos. Tequila. Arriba! Arriba!"

"Stop," I said, laughing, despite myself. "Let's continue this in my room."

"Yes, ma'am," Dylan replied eagerly. We pulled ourselves from the pool and began to shuffle back to my room, shivering and drawing a few questioning looks as we went by, soaking wet and fully clothed. Dylan couldn't pass up the opportunity to embarrass me.

"Don't mind us," Dylan said to the elderly couple goggling after us. "She had a temper tantrum and threw me in." I hit Dylan on the shoulder for that, but Dylan just added, "She didn't think I'd take her in with me. Serves her right." They winked at the couple as we passed.

Dylan and I had adjoining rooms, but it was clear now that the extra room would not be needed. Once inside, Dylan rushed to attend to my needs. They ran to the bathroom to grab us both towels and robes. A giant hot tub dominated the room, just a few feet from the king-size bed and across from a stylish seating area with tables and sofas. Dylan didn't even ask but went directly to the hot tub and began filling it.

"Can I get you out of these wet things while the hot tub fills?"

Their short dark hair was wet and clinging to their face in the sexiest way. They looked as excited as I was at the prospect of enjoying the evening together, and for the first time, I really relaxed into this thing that I knew—now—was happening. I let them undress me. Offered myself over silently, trusting, as they peeled layer after layer of clothing, each more intimate than the last, until I stood only in my heels before them.

"You're…spectacular," Dylan whispered.

I smiled and stepped forward to begin undressing them

button by button. They helped, unable, it seemed, to allow me to perform this simple task. But in the end, they stood before my gaze just as unflinchingly, awaiting my appraisal.

I'd never been with anyone with a body like mine. I was uncertain what to do, and yet moved by the interplay of sameness and difference between us.

"You're...beautiful. Handsome? I'm not sure what to call you," I admitted.

"As long as you like what you see, you can call me whatever you like," they said, pulling me in for a lengthy kiss. We cracked open the complimentary bottle of champagne and moved to the hot tub. On the wall opposite, over a trendy couch, there was a giant, circular mirror that was lit up from behind. We turned off all the lights save that one and sank into the tub's warm depths. Its heat was a wonderful sensation after our chilly walk of shame.

We kissed some more, Dylan's tongue exploring my mouth forcefully. I wrapped my legs around them and relaxed into the sensations, familiar but long forgotten, of real desire. The ledge of the tub was slanted, and so we had to place our drinks on a little table beside the tub. Dylan got up to reach for the glasses, and I took advantage of the opportunity to press my body against theirs, pushing them up against the far edge of the tub, staring at our figures in the mirror. I kissed Dylan's neck, and they leaned back, a little moan escaping their throat. I liked how we looked together, and I traced my manicured nails along the swell of their chest uncertainly. They hung their head and pushed back into me, so I figured it was good. But I wasn't sure how to proceed.

"I'm not really sure what to do," I admitted, feeling a weird mixture of embarrassment and elation. The mirror was getting to me. There was no hiding that I was being outrageous. But then I didn't want to hide it. I wanted to watch it. To revel in it. To see just how far I would go.

"Follow your pleasure," Dylan replied. "There are no rules."

And so I let my hands trace Dylan's outlines, watching all the while in the mirror. Dylan grabbed a glass and drank while I explored, never taking their eyes off me in the mirror. When I moved my hand between their legs, they widened their stance in a manner refreshingly frank and inviting. I'd never touched anyone's vulva before, so I was surprised at how naturally I set to work pleasing them. It felt right. Electric. I figured they must like the same things I did. And it appeared they did, for they closed their eyes and growled their pleasure quite openly. I touched their folds, soft and wet, as my mind kept repeating the ludicrous imaginary headline from earlier. Tawdry Queer Sex Scandal. *Tawdry. Queer. Sex.* Except rather than filling me with shame or dread, the words seemed to egg me on.

I'd spent my whole life being good. Trying to live up to the demands of my station. But not now. Not in this moment. This was for me. And Dylan. They grabbed my hand and pushed hard on my fingers, forcing me to place a great deal of pressure on their clit. I took the hint and increased my pace and force. They pushed their weight back into me, and I pushed them forward, against the edge of the tub, which was sloshing now with the tempo of our lovemaking.

No, actually, not lovemaking. Nothing that saccharine. This was more animal than that. Fierce. Undeniable. Raw. Dylan growled and reached back to grab my hair and pull me close. Then they hunched and let out a long moan as their whole body spasmed, letting go of my hair and clutching the sides of the tub for support as the waves of orgasm rocked their body. It was spectacular, truly a sight to see. And I genuinely felt powerful, having inspired such evident pleasure in someone.

"Holy shit, woman," Dylan said, falling back into the tub like a rag doll, panting and momentarily spent.

I laughed, the joy just bubbling out of me.

"Come here," Dylan said, inviting me to lie back and rest against them in the water. I positioned myself, snuggling atop them, and just enjoyed the effervescence of the water and the feelings coursing inside me, novel and invigorating. Dylan petted my hair as their breathing slowly returned to normal.

"Damn, and here I thought I was gonna show you a good time and cater to *your* needs."

"There's still time for that," I teased.

"Indeed," they replied, shifting positions so that our mouths could meet once more.

"I've had enough of the tub, if that's okay with you."

"Your wish is my command, m'lady."

Dylan shut off and drained the tub while I moved to the bed, awaiting them with eager anticipation.

"How can I please you? Name it and it's yours," they offered, when at last they came to join me on the giant bed.

I answered without hesitation: "I want to ride your face."

I'd seen that once in a dirty movie my husband had shown me in our early days. At the time, it had struck me as unspeakably vulgar. I had always been really restrained and uncertain in bed. In fact, my husband had once complained that I was too quiet, so I'd try to make some noise, but it always felt forced and unnatural. Now I wanted to try it with this amazing person who made me feel free and more than just a little wild.

Dylan eagerly complied. And I discovered I could be noisy when it felt right. Which it did. Over and over again. On Dylan's cock. On their fist. On their face. In the shower. In the rental car. In the moonlit ocean. Over and over again for months. Until Dylan left to go tree planting in Northern Ontario, and our short-lived but well-enjoyed "arrangement" was over. But until then…over and over. In the garden. On the dining room table. Over and over.

So. Many. Fucks. Given.

PART TWO: LOVERS IN A DANGEROUS TIME
DYSTOPIAN EROTICA

GODDESS COMPLEX

I am known by many names. The Lady. She Who Gives. Shaker. Receiver of the Slain. The One Who Makes the Sea Swell. Possessor of the Brisingamen. Not to mention the unspeakable names Loki hypocritically calls me.

Mostly I am known as Freyja the Beautiful. Of course. Women are always reduced to their bodies. The skalds sing epics in honor of Odin's wisdom, Thor's strength, and Loki's cunning, but of the goddesses, we hear nothing but praise for our looks. Luckily, I am cunning enough to know I need not boast of my wisdom or strength, both of which I recognize I will need in full force if I am to survive what is upon us.

Like the All-Father, I know the signs. Odin had to go to a seer for the knowledge. I am a seer. I brought Vanir magick to the Aesir, but Odin is blind in more ways than one. And so Ragnarok begins. But it will not be the twilight of *all* the gods. It will not be the end of me and mine.

At least, not all of mine. Alas, some fates are decreed, and no magick can undo the cruel dictates of a malevolent Norn, so I have mourned my twin brother's death in silence for years. I cannot interfere with his destiny or the destiny of so many of my fellow deities—friends and past lovers—doomed to perish in this immense battle foretold to upturn the worlds. Even my daughters' births were laced with the grief of foreknowledge of their deaths at Ragnarok. I knew from the moment they first suckled how I would lose them.

Tempting though it is to fight fate, I am not fool enough to hope I can outwit the Norns, the fortune-giving entities that oversee us all. Even gods have limits to their fearsome powers. But I am a sorceress. I weave the forces of existence too. And the visions showed me one great love that would not be taken from me if I used my powers cunningly. I focus on this battle alone.

Ragnarok is upon us. I feel it in my flesh. Soon Heimdall will raise his mighty horn and herald its arrival for all the gods to hear. The world tree will shudder, and the battle will begin. Today is the prophesied day where worlds collide and are destroyed. But today is also the day where I am fated to attempt to save the one woman who has become my entire world.

❖

"You beckoned, Fair One?" Sigvalda strides into the bedchamber, unbuckling leather and armor as she approaches. Her cheeks are flushed, and wisps of flaming hair that escaped her braid stick to her sweaty forehead. She smells earthy, of horse and combat.

"The day has scarcely begun. Have you been training already?"

"You know I like to start the day with a brisk morning ride. I ran into Hildegunn, and we tussled for a bit. She's fierce with a spear, that one."

"So I hear."

Sigvalda removes the last of her battle gear and gazes fixedly at me, longing already evident in her gorgeous green eyes. "What do you want of me?" she asks, a smile teasing the corners of her lips.

I cross the room to fuss over her clothing, straightening

her shirt and tidying her hair. "You're quite the mess, as usual," I cluck.

"And you are feminine perfection embodied, as usual," she retorts, stilling my hands by grabbing them to pull me into a hungry embrace.

I have loved many beings in my lifetime. My lips have pressed to many others. But no one's kisses have stirred me as profoundly as hers. I've often wondered what it is about her that makes her so unique, for whether elf, human, giantess, deity, or dwarf, no one has equaled this Valkyrie in passion and stamina. Always, my lovers have disappointed me. They are ever sated before me and leave me hungry. Until Sigvalda.

Loki likes to accuse me loudly and publicly of excess and perversion, but this is sexist hypocrisy coming from someone who regularly changes species and sex to father monstrous bastards upon the worlds. I sleep with whoever I choose. His puritanical crowing was ear splitting when he heard how I earned the Brisingamen, the most beautiful treasure in existence, a necklace so wondrous that its name means "the jewel whose fire cannot be resisted." I could not resist; I had to have it. But there was no treasure greater than it to trade for it. I asked the four dwarves who crafted it to name their price. A night with each of them seemed a fair price for such a treasure. And not without its pleasures, however physically repugnant they might have seemed. I've never been inflexible when it comes to ideas of right and wrong.

But Sigvalda *is* inflexible in her moral code. Her sense of honor and loyalty would keep her here through the great battle. She would fight and die for Odin without question. So I must stop her by any deception necessary. She may never forgive me for it, but she will live to be angry with me about it, and that must be enough.

I can only pray that my charms are sufficiently potent.

I pull away from her searching kiss, inspiring a low growl in her throat as she reluctantly releases me.

I smile and begin to weave another spell. "I beckoned you here because I intend to make love to you as never before. Today, I will earn my title as the goddess of love. Sound enticing?" I ask, eyebrow raised coyly.

Another growl as she pulls me closer, strong arms encircling my waist. "It would be pretty hard to top what happened at Ifing River," she says.

"That won't even make the top ten of our erotic encounters after today," I add, wiggling closer to nuzzle into her neck and nibble on her ear. I feel her body quiver in immediate response.

"Better than that time on your chariot?" she murmurs as a hand slips down to grab and knead my bottom.

"So much better," I assure her, using my warm breath to tickle her ear.

"What about the time we invited Idunn to join us?" she asks, both hands now firmly cupping my cheeks and drawing me to her pelvis.

"That was nothing," I say breathily before trailing gentle kisses down the slope of her neck. I stop and look her full in the face. "I'm going to make love to you as if it's the end of the world. You best not have any plans today because once we begin, you are not leaving this room until you've experienced multiple, earth-shattering orgasms. Do you consent?"

A brilliant smile illuminates her face, and I know my magick is begun.

❖

I take her to my bathing hall, which is all marble, steam, and greenery. I busy myself adding oils and herbs to the bath while she watches me work, leaning suggestively against a wall, following my every curve and movement. She likes to look at me, as I suppose most do. I am not called Freyja the Fair for nothing. The Viking poets make much of my ice blue eyes and golden tresses. Add to this the Brisingamen that shimmers alluringly on my neck, its ever-shifting flames of colors casting light from my delicate collarbone. Yes, beauty is a power familiar to me. To intensify this power on this critical day, I wear nothing but an elegantly simple white gown with gilded clasps and embroidery to match my flaxen hair. It's somewhat sheer, and I'm very much aware that it will become more translucent in the steam and moisture of this room. Judging from Sigvalda's smirk and focused stare, she's very much aware as well.

"Your bath awaits," I offer, posing flirtatiously on a cushion by the side of the sunken tub. Sigvalda removes her clothing slowly, never breaking eye contact with me, for I suppose I like to look at her too. And as always, I like what I see. Her skin is fair and rosy, her frame tall and stately like mine but much more athletic and compact. I am curvy where she is toned. As she strides toward me, I note how her breasts are pert, her stomach tight, and her thighs strong. I offer her my hand for balance as she steps in to the wet warmth of the bath. She closes her eyes to sigh with pleasure, and I can feel the rush of heat that engulfs her body. It brings me pleasure too.

I attend to her body, starting by unraveling the striking scarlet braid that contains her long, lush mane of hair. I shake the tresses free and briefly massage her scalp of any discomfort from the braid and her helmet. She slips under the water to emerge a moment later, dripping and grinning. I beckon her back to me, pouring cleanser into my palms. She obeys and settles in against the side of the tub, allowing me to wash her hair. I lather the cleanser well and use my strong hands to thoroughly scrub her scalp. I know she loves the sensation so I draw it out, massaging forcefully and rhythmically. I smile as I watch the simple sensual pleasure register on her face. I use a jug to rinse her hair, pouring carefully, controlling the flow thoughtfully. I feel this in my flesh too. The warm, wet rush of the water spilling over the crown of my head. I pour more times than strictly necessary, just for the sensation of it. Then I work conditioner into the length of her locks, pampering her tresses with scented moisturizers. I rinse once more, then get up to find a sponge.

When I turn back to the tub, she is floating with her chin resting atop her arms crossed over the tub edge closest to me. She watches me wolfishly, and I laugh, realizing she is already hungry for more amatory sensual pleasure.

"Why don't you join me in here?" she asks, rakishly raising an eyebrow.

"You're still a very dirty battle-maiden come from riding and sparring. Let's clean you first," I answer, smiling and settling beside the tub once more.

"Well, I am very dirty, that's true," she drawls suggestively. "But your idea doesn't sound nearly as much fun as dirtying you up too." Sigvalda splashes me playfully, and I feign annoyance, looking down with mock reproach at how my nipples are now clearly showing through the thin fabric of my wet gown.

"Bath first. Love later," I reply sternly.

"Love always comes first, my lady," Sigvalda says, hastening from the water's grasp to pull me, squealing and struggling, into the bath alongside her.

"Sig! You beast!"

My protests are short-lived, however, for Sigvalda's touch is exquisitely alchemical, transforming the energy of my resistance to the energy of excitement. To the universal, erotic energy of playful pursuit, struggle and submission. And this is the secret heart of sex: *energy*. Most feel it. Some intuit its power. Few can fully harness its potency. If there's one reason why I am worshiped as a goddess of love, I suspect it is not so much due to my beauty as to my possession of this secret and the skill to wield it. Sorceresses weave spells with energies. I know how to channel the primal desires that inspire all life to union. I can tune into my lover's feelings and experience them myself. I can project my own sensations or inspiration into my more receptive lovers. They may simply sense it, or it may present as unbidden imagery that leaps to mind in the throes of passion, whether it is the energy of searing lava exploding from a boiling caldera or of thirsty young greenery relieved by the gift of morning's dew. Perhaps sunflowers following the warmth of the sun's shifting face. Stallions, strong and muscled, galloping fiercely across a plain. Or cats grooming one another at ease in a sunbeam. All of these are energies of life's desire. They can be called upon.

In the moment, Sigvalda and I are wet heat, slippery and surging. We are sultry and moist. We play at embodying pirate and sea witch at storm. I wrap my legs about her and allow my hips to gyrate in rhythm with our warm, teasing breath. She steals kisses as I undulate before her. The waters of the bath heave to our motion. They spill over the sides, splashing the floors, making them as slick as ourselves. I live up to my title, making the seas swell all right.

"I must have you," she growls, biting my shoulder lightly.

I chuckle and pull myself up out of the rolling waves we created. I stand with regal posture before her in the tub, naked and streaming, with my sex ripe and on offer before her face. She doesn't hesitate, accepting with an eager mouth.

Ah, Sigvalda. Her tongue is practiced, her motions knowing. We have loved each other long by now, and the sweet familiarity adds comfort. More than any of my previous lovers, even my flighty ex-husband, we are right together. Her tongue creates a lovely, lulling cadence on my sex while her strokes on my torso, behind, and breasts add variety and punch. She plays me like an instrument; I quiver and sound to her commands. A finger slips inside me, then two—or is it three—creating new and urgent notes. The tempo rises, crescendo nears. She grasps the Brisingamen, tugging slightly, grasping tightly as her mouth holds steady pressure on my clit, and her fingers dart within me steadily, insistently.

My legs begin to tremble. I savor the sensation here, right on the edge of spilling over. I draw it out as long as I can stand it, literally, until I collapse in a climactic splash that sends a deluge across the bath chamber floor. I cling to my lover fiercely as the spasms rock my body. In time with each ripple of pleasure, I murmur her sweet name.

When I open my eyes once more, Sigvalda's gaze is fixed joyfully on mine.

"Is it just me, or is the great hall of Sessrumnir shaking?" she asks.

"Oh, it's just the earth-shattering orgasms I promised you. You know, the ones that *you* somehow ended up delivering to *me*," I lie, laughing.

She joins in the laughter, pulling me in close for more soulful kissing. I kiss her, but my mind is elsewhere, pondering the fragility of this deception. The powerful, protective shell I cast about the hall is wavering. She does not know it, but outside our love nest, this world is ending. The sun has gone black, and the sky has split. As foretold, Loki has turned traitor. The earth quakes, the oceans storm, and perhaps the rainbow bridge has already collapsed. Frost giants have no doubt invaded by now. The gods are battling in futility. All this is raging outside, the legendary end of days for Odin's reign, and yet inside my enchanted cocoon, there is naught but oblivion. I notice the runes ritually painted on my flesh begin to shine, and I rush to move us back to the bedchamber, deeper inside the hall's protection.

❖

"Another of your love potions?" Sigvalda asks.

"The mead of poetry," I reply, holding a cup before her.

"So…a love potion."

"Of sorts. It will heighten perception. Deepen impact. Loosen our tongues."

"In that case, bottoms up." Sigvalda tips the cup to her lips and swallows deeply. I take but a sip of my own cup, determined to remain sober and alert though in tune to Sigvalda's more intoxicated experience.

We are in my bedchamber now. I wear a silken bathing robe in a wintry blue to match my eyes. Sigvalda wears nothing. She is bold in her body and enjoys showing it off for me. I step closer to her and place my hand at the bottom of her cup, tipping it up, encouraging her to drain its contents. She complies and waits to see what I will do next. In answer, I nuzzle into her body, and we begin to sway to our own unique, intrinsic rhythm. Everything else falls away. I feel her attune and melt into me. Only then do I whisper in her ear.

"I desire to dance for you. Will you watch me?"

She moans in response and pulls me closer, grinding her pelvis against mine.

"Go to the bed. Do as I command."

Sometimes, she resists my control, but today, she merely gives a crooked smile and plods off to the huge four-poster that dominates the room. She tugs open the bed curtains and throws herself down amidst the many pillows. Her hands lace behind her head, and she eyes me with contentment and daring.

"Let the show begin," she says.

"For your viewing pleasure, brave Valkyrie."

I conjure leisurely, hypnotic music full of sexy and soulful sounds. I close my eyes and allow its rhythms to compel movement in my famously delectable frame. I took but a sip of the mead, yet I feel the resonances deep in my flesh, so I realize she must feel them even more vividly. My body responds to the notes effortlessly. I wave my hips, caress my own curves, linger and lavish attention. I make eye contact with Sigvalda, whose own hands have already wandered between her thighs.

I play with my hair and turn my back to her, the better to lose myself in sensation. I undulate with the beat. Grab the trim of my silken robe and rhythmically edge it up, up, over the deliciously rounded curve of my buttocks. Let the hem fall. Twirl around to assess her reaction. Note the already steadfast tempo of her fingers and smile. I trace my own fingers along the curvature of my neck to my décolletage and place my hand inside my robe to grasp my breast. I tweak my own nipple, aware that Sigvalda is radiating envy of my touch. She is ever eager to lay hands on me. I allow one breast to peep out. Show her how I like it caressed. Revel in messing with what I know to be her irrational compulsion for symmetry. She wants me to reveal my other breast. She needs me to do it. Do it. Do it now. But I won't. I deny her both symmetry and touch. I just watch her squirm.

"Come closer," she says, sitting up. "Let me touch you."

"You wish," I tease, sashaying away from her.

"Freyja! Come here. Please."

"I'll come close, but no touching. Hold the posts at the edge of the bed and don't let go. Understood?"

Sig throws back her head and groans.

"Understood?"

She rolls her eyes and grasps the end posts with dramatic exasperation.

I dance my way to her. Press my body against hers, then take it away but keep it oh-so-enticingly, frustratingly close. I tantalize her with silk and flesh, connecting and withdrawing in time with the music's dips and swells.

Then I bring myself close to her and press my soft lips to hers. The tips of our tongues meet, touching ever so timorously. We explore sweetly with our mouths for a time until I break away and ask, "Would you like me to disrobe?"

"Is Thor fond of his hammer?" She smiles at the obviousness of her assent. I smile back, then brusquely yank the bed curtains shut on her.

"What the...Freyja!"

Sigvalda makes to open the curtains, but I respond sternly,

"I told you not to let go of the posts. Be a good warrior and do what you're told."

"Maybe on the battlefield, but you know that I have never been capable of that in the bedchamber," Sigvalda reminds me from behind the sheer fabric.

"I know. But your struggle amuses me, so endure it."

I unlace the single strand of silk that keeps my body hidden from her. I let the loosened garment fall luxuriously from my shoulders, down my torso and legs to the floor. I continue to sway and beckon, conscious that I am all shapes and shadow to my beloved behind the diaphanous curtain. I move. Let the music enter and become part of me. I twirl away and come spinning back. I press myself to the translucence of the fabric separating us. Just hold myself there to feel the rising insistence of touch building in both of us.

"Beloved, please," she moans. I can feel both our hearts beating in tandem. Our panting breath mingles through the cloth. The tension is perfect. I slowly pull the curtain halfway open. Our eyes meet with smoldering intensity.

"Please touch me," Sigvalda says.

"Lie back."

She obeys, all but vibrating with desire. Having tormented her so mercilessly in the lead-up, I waste no time giving her her heart's desire. I bring my mouth to her and find her already fired with longing. The mead must be powerful indeed. I dance with my tongue, breath, and lips now, making music with my mouth. Sigvalda moans and speaks her desire more brazenly than ever before.

"You're so exquisite, Freyja. I want to come all over your magnificent face. So beautiful. Your face. Your smile. Your hair…"

Her thoughts freed by the mead, she repeats herself and voices her worship of my beauty as my mouth attests to my worship of hers.

"Your breasts. Your belly. Your hips," she murmurs.

I assess her readiness and fill her with my fingers. Her whole body quakes in response, and everything shifts hot and fast between us. She bucks and thrashes while I keep a steady beat. She grasps my hair and locks my face in close, thrusting her hips with urgent need. I feel her furious yearning suffuse me. I feel her sex open more profoundly, revealing hidden layers of desirous space, so I fill them generously and vigorously. I bid her open for me. I demand more of her secret self, and she provides, opening and opening depths of herself that she didn't even know she had. She starts to shudder and spill over, cursing colorfully like only a battle warrior can, and I hold her steady through the tumult. I hold her steady as she breaks apart in the inexpressibly gorgeous and miraculous manner in which good love undoes and then recreates a person.

"I love you," she cries, over and over like a mantra. "I love you. I love you."

But each utterance is a knife blade. Will she ever profess it again once she knows? I am trying to keep her protected until the last possible, hopeless moment, but I can't keep it from her much longer. The runes glow brighter. The moment upon which her uncertain fate rests draws nearer.

❖

"I have a gift for you."

"I need no gift but you," Sigvalda counters.

I insist. "It is something only I have possessed until now." She looks at me confused, and I leave the warmth of the bed to return to her with my offering. It's a cloak of falcon feathers, exactly like my own.

She springs up, mouth agape, unable to speak.

"Come fly with me."

Sigvalda leaps from the bed and practically tackles me to the floor, she is so excited. This is a gift beyond reckoning.

Rare and magickal. Were she not the love of my life and were this not the end of days, I would not have paid the price I did to acquire it. As it stands, her amusingly exuberant gratitude is recompense enough. Never mind that it will fortify her chances of survival.

"Allow me," I say, holding out the cloak. I wrap it about her shoulders, and the enchanted bonds fasten. I step back to behold her properly. The russet feathers bring out the auburn of her hair atop and below, as well as the tender salmon tan of her nipples. She is transformed to a charmed creature, half woman, half bird. I've never worn the cloak in the nude before, but clearly, I should have tried it, for the effect is spellbinding. The feathered wings shield then reveal her undress as she tries her wings. Her feet hover off the ground, and she hoots in excitement. I grab my own cloak and join her.

"Like this," I say, showing her the motions that best control flight. She's a quick study, and it's not long before we are both floating by the ceiling as awed laughter pours from Sigvalda's throat.

"Try to keep up," I call, leading her through the door and up to the sparring chamber, which has the highest ceilings in my hall. Her motions are uncertain and jerky at first, but she manages to follow. The next while is me teaching her tricks. At times, we laugh and banter together in noisy joy, zooming about the hall. We chase, plummet, and wheel about the massive space, just reveling in the incomparable pleasures of flight. At other times, we glide and soar together in wordless companionship, in that comfortable silence that is the hallmark of true intimacy. Sigvalda is an athlete and battle maiden with exceptional physical mastery, so she catches on quickly, experimenting with the prospects and limits of her new cloak.

As she becomes more comfortable and confident, new possibilities for the cloak appear to cross Sigvalda's mind. She flutters close to me, her hair blowing about becomingly in the drafts from our wingbeats. She presses her body to mine, eyebrow arched. I smile and throw my leg about her shoulder. Our sexes meet in midair. We bob and dip, her mound to mine, flame and sunshine. We circle and rise, up, up, circle and rise to the ceiling, a grinding, groaning, fluttering mass of flesh and feathers. Our lips below kiss and part, rub and grind as our powerful wings keep us swirling aloft. It's like nothing I've experienced. A few more mighty wingbeats, and we concentrate all our force on the union of our places of power, our sexes soft and wet and eager for each other. A few more mighty wingbeats, then in the heady freedom of flight, we orgasm together, crashing clumsily to the ground after our incredible airborne ecstasy.

"That was…amazing," Sigvalda stammers, eyes ablaze with enthusiasm and awe.

I disentangle myself, note the brilliance of my runes and quickly check the huge floor-to-ceiling windows to gauge the strength of the illusion spell that keeps her from seeing what I do not wish her to see. Already, the spell wavers. The glass flickers. Dread courses through me as I consider how much time remains. The hall is vibrating. She will notice soon. I can't distract her forever.

Oblivious still, Sigvalda asks, "Why don't you ever fight in your cloak?" She grabs a sword from the wall to try her hand at aerial combat.

"It's possible but tricky. You need both arms free to beat the air most effectively. I prefer my chariot."

"Yeah, but if you practiced, you could perform some wicked dive strikes," she muses, flying high, then plunging rapidly, blade-first. She lands gracefully. "What's with the ritual runes? You hardly need to use sex magick to seduce me, sweetling."

Then her brow furrows. Her eyes go to her feet, then along the floor to the windows. She strides quickly to the glass.

"Something's off. Freyja, do you see this? The hall really is shaking."

As she speaks, the spell falters, and the outside world is faintly visible for the minutest moment. It's enough. Like every Valkyrie, Sigvalda has prepared all her life for this battle. She races on foot for the great oaken doors that lead to the fields. Then she flies. She struggles to remove the enormous plank that blocks the door from outside entry. It's a job meant for many powerful arms working in tandem. She curses and begins angrily hacking at the plank instead.

I breathe deeply, call for the flying cats that pull my chariot, climb aboard, and pause. I see Sigvalda change her mind and turn to find an easier exit. Fear courses through my veins, not so much at the state of this world, which I have seen in the visions innumerable times, but at the uncertainty of Sigvalda's fate. Her murky destiny hinges on her reaction to this moment, a reaction I could never see because it was never decided. Once in an odd moon, a Norn is neglectful, and a soul's end is not foretold. Such is the fortuitous case with Sigvalda. Her Norn's carelessness is my opportunity. When I see her flying for another way out, I brace myself, gather my power, and voice the ancient incantation to unbind this most potent of spells.

The windows explode in a maelstrom of broken glass, howling wind, and surging water. The chariot lurches sideways as my great cats struggle with the sudden tempest. Shielding my eyes from the blustering wind and blinding spray, I spot Sigvalda fighting with the elements to stay upright and afloat in air, for the hall is rapidly filling with murky, swirling water. She is using the sword to hack fingerholds into the wall, edging her way to one of the broken windows.

I urge my mighty beasts toward my beloved, who strains with ferocious determination toward a gusting hole of shattered pane. With admirable grit, she pulls herself outside before I can reach her. The window is too narrow for my chariot, so I use a spell to disintegrate the oaken door. More water rushes in, and we wait for the first deadly rush to subside, then swim through and out. My drenched felines shake the water from their fur and strain under my reins. It takes all my powers of command to keep them from fleeing this sinking world.

Sigvalda first. We careen about the rapidly drowning remains of Sessrumnir, my longtime home on Asgard, the world that once was the domain of the Aesir gods. I cannot spy Sigvalda anywhere. She just acquired the cloak. Will it be enough to give her the edge on this apocalyptic gale? We race about blindly in the squall. I catch a flash of reddish brown from the corner of my eye and whirl the chariot about wildly. It's her. Grasping a piece of the great, unfinished wall that surrounds Asgard, the one that was supposed to protect us from the frost giants and other would-be invaders. The one that is currently crumbling. We race toward her.

"Sig, give me your hand," I shout into the wind. "We can still make it to Vanaheim. The home of the Vanir gods will welcome you."

Sigvalda doesn't speak. She isn't even looking at me, though my chariot is hovering precariously beside her, fighting gale-force winds to await her.

"Sigvalda! Please!"

She does not or will not hear. She merely stares at the ruins of this once-thriving planet and says nothing. I have forgotten the immensity of this scene. It is not that I am untouched by the carnage, but I have seen it so many times in my visions that it has lost much of its raw power. I've mourned it for so long. Ragnarok's dead were gone for me years ago, though they walked with me still. For Sigvalda, the scope of the slaughter and annihilation is overwhelming.

I watch in agony as tears fill her eyes. She is a Valkyrie. She trained the valiant and glorious dead for this final clash. She prepared her entire life for this battle. And I stole it from her. To steal her from death, I think in desperate justification. I reach my hand to her. A hand that has loved her in countless, cherished ways.

"Sigvalda, my father awaits us in my home world. We will be safe there. We can live our days in peace. Just take my hand."

Her face contorts in rage, and I fear I have misjudged her, that she may throw herself into the abyss out of her misguided sense of loyalty and honor. My mind is racing for a spell to bind her to me when she speaks at last in a quiet voice that I hear with uncanny clarity amidst the deafening tumult: "How can I ever forgive you?"

Her eyes meet mine, and it is a look, the import and weight of which I will live with forever. It sears her feelings of fury and betrayal into my very bones. It is a look that binds us frozen in the fullness of a tortured love that compelled such desperate treachery. We gaze at one another in the whirling chaos of a dying planet. We gaze at each other as embodiments of accusation and supplication, battling one another in the ruins of a war to end a realm.

In the downpour, in the raging maelstrom of the most intense feelings and the most devastating elements, the world died, and our love did not. She took my hand.

❖

Of course, no one ever sang this epic. Women's stories are never told as we would tell them. What lives on of me in Norse tales of old are countless silly tales of how Loki tried to marry me off to this or that stranger as part of this or that shady ruse. All because Freyja the Fair was so beautiful that every living creature desired her. Now that may or may not be true, but I believe it just might be the least interesting thing about me.

My name has all but fallen away. The stars named for my dress have become known by another god's name. Freyja's gown has become Orion's belt. That is the way of things. Dynasties rise and fall. And women, most of all, disappear. But that is not such a serious thing. Mortals know me still. We meet in the throes of intimate ecstasy. In the jittery rush of first love. In the unspeakably deep contentment of a newborn's suckling. Few speak my name. But many feel my power.

If it matters not that my name is falling away, however, then I must ask myself why voice this tale at all? Perhaps it is because for so many planetary turns, I have listened to others tell the story of Freyja, the fertility goddess of the North. Perhaps you recognize her: Freyja, twin sister of Frey, of whom much more is known. Freyja, promiscuous temptress, the most desired of all beings. Freyja, dutiful mother and wife, the slut redeemed.

Perhaps, just once, I wanted to voice my own story. To tell a tale that was focused less on my flesh as a promise of pleasure and meaning to others and more as a locus of pleasure and meaning for myself.

See, my domain, like all women's, is love. In that, we can be powerful. In that, we can presume control. But only because it's deemed frivolous and sentimental. In our little queendom of supposed inconsequence, it's all bodies and babies, weddings and mindless rutting. These things can be ours. But they're all we can be. At least in their stories.

I am more than my body. And yet, my body is my greatest source of power and wisdom. This queendom I was granted out of sheer contempt and dismissal, this domain we call love, it is the most vital and profound of the realms. It is all that matters in the end. And I've lived through a prophesied end of days, so you can take my words for wisdom.

I tell you my story because if I've learned one thing in all the vast expanse of time that I have lived on multiple worlds, it is this: When a great love lies within your grasp, you must use all your powers to save it. Given a chance at true love, at changing or saving the life of a beloved, you must use all your strengths to do so. And we are all powerful. We are all magick. Energies can always be called upon. *I continue to exist.* Sorceress that I am, I lived through the twilight of the gods. You can still—and forever and always—call on me. Freyja, the wise, strong, and cunning.

FIRST CONTACT

Laid Eyes

I knew I was fucked the moment I laid eyes on her. What the hell was a white woman doing this far north squatting in my family's hunting shack? Well, I guess I knew what she was literally doing, and I should have looked away, but I couldn't take my eyes off her. She was naked, standing in my kitchen, using water boiled on the wood stove to sponge bathe her body. I'd spotted the smoke quite a ways off and came prepared to take on whatever threat had found my hideaway. I wasn't prepared for her, though.

She was blond. No one this far north was blond. At least not above *and* below. Sure, some of the reservation bimbos tried to fake it with expensive chemical dyes, but blond was something foreign and exotic that we only ever saw on TV and the internet. Back when those things still existed.

I knew I was being a creeper, but still I looked on, her body framed by the window as she used a cloth to wash her tall, lithe frame. She had an angry looking rash on her left calf, but otherwise, she was physically perfect. I didn't check out her eye color, but her skin was pale, and her tits were small with perky pink nipples. Her hips were soft curves, and her ass was perfectly rounded. There was soft, ample fuzz of the lightest shade of tan between her thighs.

I felt like I'd stumbled into some strange pornographic movie because nothing this extraordinarily sexy had ever happened to me before. She was scrubbing the length of her arms, then her tits and torso, and I felt my own sex get slick at the way her rosy little nipples tightened up. I squirmed and thought about touching myself, but that was a step too far for my dignity. I snapped back into the reality of the situation, which was that a stranger was trying to steal my home. And even if she was a startlingly gorgeous stranger, she was still a threat.

I retreated to the trees and walked full-circle around the house, looking for clues. Who was she? Was she alone? Did she have weapons? What did she want? I snuck up to the other windows and peered inside. She seemed to be traveling solo. And light. But looks could be deceiving, especially nowadays. It was at least five days' hike back to the reserve. I weighed out whether I should return later to confront her with reinforcements but decided to stick it out and spy on her for a full day. See what I could glean about this mysterious white woman with her golden locks.

Finders Keepers

Somewhere along the way, time had stopped being meaningful. I couldn't tell how many days I had been running. Just as I couldn't tell where I was. Probably months. Definitely north. I only knew that because I'd been in cottage country in Northern Ontario when the war began. We didn't even know who was responsible, but everyone seemed to agree that it was an EMP, which I quickly learned was an electromagnetic pulse designed to cripple a country's infrastructure, taking out the electrical grid and all tech. But who the hell would want to target Canada? We'd all thrown around wild guesses in the early days, back when people stuck together and looked to each other for answers and support. Maybe it was Russia. Maybe it was North Korea. Maybe it was supposed to hit the US. Maybe it had. We had no way of knowing.

I knew I was heading north, though, because when things fell spectacularly apart and I realized that people were no longer safe to be around, I'd packed light but smart. One of my precious few possessions was a compass that had been lying around the cottage. I didn't know exactly why it gave me comfort but it did. Maybe because I knew that if I just kept heading north, I would encounter fewer and fewer people. Maybe because with it, I knew how to reverse my course to find my way home should the time ever come when it was safe to do so. Maybe I just liked the idea of knowing where I was going in a literal sense, when I had absolutely no clue where I was going in a deeper sense. There were so many unanswered questions. So I just ran. Always north. Just me and my pack. Scavenging along the way.

Stumbling onto this shack was a godsend. At first, I was finding cottages, then hunting shacks fairly regularly. I'd scout them out, make sure they were empty, then raid them for supplies. Stay a few days. Keep running. Movement helped me not to overthink. *Just put one foot in front of the other, Emmeline. Don't think about what you left behind. Don't remember what happened when things turned ugly.*

The problem was that winter was fast approaching. I was seriously rethinking my impulse to head north when I stumbled on this particular shack, the first one I had seen in weeks. It was tiny but tidy and well stocked. I was considering whether it would be wise to hole up here for the winter when I somehow knew that I wasn't alone. I couldn't explain it, except as a survival instinct. I sauntered casually to my pack, acting as though nothing were amiss, then grabbed the handgun I had stolen from my idiotic ex-boyfriend. I made sure my back was to the wall as I carefully began sweeping the rooms for intruders like I'd seen in countless cop flicks.

She was standing in the open front door, waiting for me with a rifle cocked and ready. I jumped and nearly dropped the handgun.

"We don't have to hurt each other," she said, her aim steady and her finger on the trigger. "I will if I have to, but I'd prefer not to."

I kept my gun pointed at her, but my hands were clearly shaking. Neither of us said anything for the longest time. We stood in a frozen standoff, assessing each other keenly. She was distractingly attractive, with bronzed skin, deep black eyes, and long dark hair tucked into a tidy braid. Her face was angular in a strangely compelling way that spoke of strength.

"This place is mine. You have no right to be here."

I knew she was right, but this was the first place I had considered staying after running for so long. Some rash madness in me pushed me to bluster, "It was empty when I found it. They say possession is nine-tenths of the law. Finders keepers and all that."

She gave a short, brutal laugh. "White men say that. And their time is coming to an end, it would seem."

I squirmed uncomfortably. What the hell was she talking about?

"Listen," she said, "I've been watching you since yesterday. I know you're alone, and I can tell you've never shot a gun. Why don't you stop pretending that you're going to shoot me, and I'll put my gun away too? We can talk. Figure out a way forward." She slowly lowered her rifle, never breaking eye contact.

I was relieved, for indeed, my gun didn't even have bullets.

❖

The Beginning

That first night was torture. We ate guardedly by candlelight while carefully sussing out each other's story, trading information with cautious watchfulness. Her yellow hair was aglow like a halo about her lovely face, and I couldn't help but recall the contours of her flesh that I had already seen in all their naked glory. She had no idea that I knew her body's secrets. Having such illicit knowledge gave me a pervy thrill. I felt guilty but also tingly whenever I thought about it.

Evidently, her name was Emma, short for Emmeline. She had been on the move since the EMP, but she wouldn't say much about why she was alone. Her eyes went hard, and she looked away when I asked, which said enough. I told her a sufficient amount about myself to satisfy a sense of reciprocity and nothing more. I knew I should send this woman on her way. But she seemed harmless. And truth be told, I was enamoured from the beginning.

That night, as we both settled into the adjacent bunk beds in the sleeping quarters, I couldn't stop my hand from sneakily wandering between my thighs, thinking of her pouty lips and the soft sky-blue eyes I had now taken the time to notice. Damn, she was pretty. Like a doll. *My very own Barbie doll, lost in the woods.*

How It Feels

Our first few days together were a whirlwind. I'd never met anyone like her. She was from the Anishinaabe First Nation and told me her name was Winona, which in Ojibway meant "first-born daughter." She preferred to be called Win. Never Winnie. She made that clear. Like she made all her feelings clear. She could be brutally curt at times. And so prickly about so many things. I tried to bond with her, thinking

I could perhaps win her over into letting me stay the winter, for she seemed harmless enough, if a little touchy at times. One time it got so hostile that I honestly thought she might shoot me. I used the term "apocalypse" to describe how it felt like the end of the world, and she launched into this long tirade about how the apocalypse had already happened centuries ago for indigenous people.

"What are you talking about?" I asked. "I'm talking about now. I'm just saying that the world has fallen apart. There's nothing left. Look at us."

"What are *you* talking about?" she countered. "Everything that matters is left. The world that fell apart was never the real world to begin with. Creator gave us all of this"—she gestured to the land around us—"and all your people did was exploit it for profit. Your pretty little Instagram world might have fallen apart, but that was never real anyway."

I was livid, mostly because I wanted to be able to say that I had never even had Instagram, but aspiring models lived by their Insta likes. I'd made my living by it and had always felt conflicted by it, *so fuck her for touching on a source of deep, personal ambivalence.* I got argumentative.

"You're so self-righteous. Not all of us can live in tepees and be one with nature or whatever." I shouldn't have said that. She made sure I knew.

"We don't live in tepees, you ignorant bitch. We live in substandard housing without clean water because idiots like you don't give a shit about native people and what's happening to the second-class citizens in your own goddamn country."

I stood up shakily. "Stop making this about race. I was just pointing out that the world is ending. Anyone can see that."

She stood up too and stared at me long and hard. "Your world is ending. Maybe mine is just beginning. Maybe now you know how it feels."

It was totally crazy, but in that moment, I had the first of many urges to kiss her. Her cheeks were flushed, her eyes were blazing, her chest was heaving, and she was radiating this defiant energy that drew me in. I'd never kissed a woman before. But in that moment, for the first time, I wondered how it would feel.

Practiced Fingers

I skimmed my finger along the top of the salve, feeling it soften under my warmth. After a few seconds, it began to melt ever so mildly, and the satisfying sensation made me smile, recalling my fascination with playing with hot candle wax.

"Roll up your left pant leg," I told her.

She complied, carefully folding the fabric up her exposed calf. She waited expectantly. The woodstove was pumping out heat, and the scent of burning logs filled the air of the small shack. Candles lit the room, casting flame and shadow. I would have given anything for a bottle of wine. Or some music. Instead, we listened to the logs crackle and watched each other with a mixture of wariness and curiosity tinged with what I suspected might be mutual desire.

"This is what you've been working on?" she asked, wrapping her gorgeous hair into an untidy bun and drawing my eyes to her chest as she lifted her arms above her head.

"Yes. It's a healing salve. It will help with the rash." I moved closer, cleared my throat self-consciously, and then gingerly took her leg in my hand. It was covered in fine white hair that felt soft and inviting. I massaged the salve gently onto the affected part of her skin. She was tense when I started but quickly relaxed into the sensation once she seemed to realize the soothing effect of the medicine.

"That feels amazing." She sighed, closing her eyes and exhaling.

So many dirty thoughts fought my better self in my mind. I wanted my touch to do this to her. I wondered how else I might make her loosen up and moan in pleasure. Would she be like the other girls on the reservation? What were white women into? Was she even attracted to me? Had she been with a woman before? What would bring her pleasure? I wanted to know. I wanted it so badly. But I focused on the present moment, my hands and my medicine making contact with the wounded part of her, bringing relief. It was no small thing.

She opened her eyes and looked at me. Looked directly at me in a way we hadn't really looked at each other before. Our faces were so close. Her lips were slightly parted. I wondered what would happen if I kissed her, just leaned in a little closer and brought my lips to hers. I wanted to, but I wasn't sure yet. So I left off massaging her leg and carefully screwed the cap back on the salve container with exaggerated focus.

"That should help," I muttered.

"It already has. Thank you," she whispered.

There was an awkward silence, interrupted only by the crackle of the fire and a sudden, sizzling pop from one of the logs. I was usually really comfortable in silence; it was my faithful companion most of the time. But in that moment, I felt uneasy, weighed down by the uncertainty of this growing connection.

"I notice you wear your hair in a braid a lot," Emma finally offered. "Is that a native thing?"

"Sort of. I just like that it keeps my hair out of my face, to be honest, but yeah, the elders say the three strands represent mind, body, and spirit. It's sort of traditional. There are lots of teachings about it."

"That's cool," she replied. She hadn't unfolded the fabric of her pants. She fidgeted with the rolled-up hem. "Have you ever tried a French braid?"

"No, I never learned how. Seems complicated."

"It's hard to do on yourself, but it's pretty easy on someone else. Would you let me try it on you?"

Her pretty azure eyes were glimmering. How could I say

no? Next thing I knew, she was behind me, unlacing my simple braid with nervous fingers. I felt my long hair fall about my face, and I struggled to remain calm and confident while she walked around to face me and assess the effect. I couldn't read her expression. She just stared at me for longer than seemed polite. Then she murmured, "You're actually really beautiful."

I snorted. "Thanks for sounding so surprised."

She laughed good-naturedly and prattled on, "Sorry. No. It's just that you don't do much to play up your femininity, so it can go unnoticed at first."

"I'm not sure you're making this better," I replied, narrowing my eyes.

She laughed all the more. "It's a compliment. I'm complimenting you. I don't always tell people this because they get all weird and judgy, but I do some modelling. And the top models always have this sort of surprising beauty, like you. They get the best work. I'm like everyday pretty. But that's nothing special. For the top-of-the-line work, you need something exotic or strange or striking. I think you have a striking kind of…stealth beauty," she finished, nodding to herself.

"Okay…thanks for the weirdest compliment I've ever received," I said as she moved behind me once more and set to running her fingers through my hair. She had lost the nervousness. Her hands moved deftly through my tresses, weaving them with practiced fingers. She finished and moved around once more to face me. She smiled, her face so close to mine that I could feel her breath.

"Stealth beauty," she whispered approvingly.

Two-Spirit

I was watching Win chop wood and thinking about why I'd never been attracted to a woman before. I supposed, for one thing, that they were never particularly nice to me. In my experience, women were catty and cruel to any other woman who might be a threat, and though it was conceited to say, it was also just honest to admit that I was considered by most people to be a very beautiful woman. Because of that, other women didn't like or trust me. And I guess that led me not to like or trust them either.

But it was also that I'd never met a woman like her. I watched her go about her days at the shack, gathering herbs, snaring then preparing rabbits, chopping wood, treating my rash, etcetera, and I was fascinated. She was capable and confident; she strode around and accomplished physically demanding tasks with ease. But she was also gentle and care-taking. She quietly tended to what was needed without complaint or desire of recognition. She had all the rugged, knowing qualities I found attractive in a man, and yet she was still soft and tender enough to present as feminine. I was captivated watching her move about our little world.

"Do you have family close by?" The words just popped out of my mouth without forethought.

She didn't look up from her chopping and stacking. "Yep. A few days' hard hike from here."

"So you just come here occasionally? You said this hunting shack belongs to your family, right?"

Win had been swinging and striking the wood with studied focus. She stopped to drink some water and answer properly. "I'm kind of a lone wolf," she said, grinning roguishly. "I wander around. I like exploring in the woods. Always have. Ever since I was a kid. I've got a few places I stay, but this one's best for winter." She placed another log on the chopping block and struck. "But yeah, I've got family fairly close by. I go see them on the reservation whenever I miss them or need something or whatever. How about you? Don't you have a family looking for you?"

I fiddled uncomfortably with my hair. "No, my family

and I have never been close. I just have myself. Well, I used to have Aiden. My ex-boyfriend. But that fell apart after the EMP." I waited for her to ask the inevitable question about what happened, but she didn't. She just looked at me, so I awkwardly blundered forward. "We were at his parents' cottage. Everything was fine at first. Even after the EMP, folks stuck together the first few weeks. But then…" My voice trailed off, and I tried not to remember certain things. "You probably don't know this far north. It's…wild out there. Vicious. People change. You can't trust anyone. Not even who you think *you* are." My eyes involuntarily started to well up, and Win must have noticed because she spared me the embarrassment of her continued gaze. She turned politely away and started chopping again while I regained my composure.

"I didn't even know anything had happened." She chuckled, shaking her head and graciously changing the tone of our interaction. "It's crazy, but that's how off the grid I live most of the year. I only found out when I ran into someone from a nearby reserve. Most of what happens to the south doesn't really affect us up here, and me even less so. I mostly do my own thing in the woods."

"Don't you get lonely?"

"Sometimes. But then I head to one of the nearby reserves to find me some 'adult companionship.'"

She winked when she said it, and I blushed like a schoolgirl, which was totally uncharacteristic.

"I'm quite popular whenever I show up, actually," she teased, her eyes twinkling. She was leaning her weight on the ax handle now, its head resting on the leaf-strewn ground.

"Oh, really?" I replied, arching an eyebrow playfully, enjoying this new energy sparking between us.

"Oh, yeah. I think it's safe to say that I am the sexiest two-spirit for kilometres around."

I had no idea what she was saying, but I liked the way she was saying it. "And what exactly is that? A two-spirit?"

"It's a native thing. It means I have the spirit of a man and the spirit of a woman. It's an honored role in our community."

"So...is that like gay? Or transgender? I'm confused."

"It's neither. It's its own thing. It doesn't really fit into the mainstream worldview, but it's mostly like a third gender, I guess, though it has aspects of sexuality and spirituality wrapped up in it too."

"Okay..." I said, still thoroughly confused.

"*I like women.* If that's what you really want to know," she stated, looking me full in the face and holding my gaze. "Do you?"

Anxiety, excitement, fear, and desire all rushed through me, adding to my confusion. "Me? No. Well, I don't know. I don't think they like me."

She smiled and leaned closer. "So...you've never been attracted to another woman? Never made out with one?"

My heart was beating wildly. She kept giving me this knowing look that unnerved me. Did she notice that I'd been checking her out? I mumbled something quasi-coherent about dirty dancing with girlfriends at a club, but that was about it. She nodded and looked off to the distance for a moment. When she turned back to me, a thoroughly wicked grin lit up her face in the most alluring manner.

"Well, it is the end of the world and all, so maybe you should try it." The air between us was electric with sudden sexiness. I could barely breathe for fear of breaking the spell.

I held her eyes and answered coyly. "Maybe I should."

"Maybe I should ask you on a proper apocalyptic date, then."

"Maybe you should."

She chuckled. "Okay, Emmeline Olivia Johnson, will you go to the Moose Rock hot spring with me tomorrow? It's the best make-out spot in the North. All the prettiest girls hope to be taken there."

"I'd love to," was all I could manage to get out.

❖

Occupied

We left at first light for the spring. She could not have been louder, tramping through the forest undergrowth and scaring off all the wildlife. She was also super visible in her little red hoodie. How she had managed to make it this far without encountering trouble was beyond me.

The whole time I was leading the way to the spring, I kept wishing that she was walking in front of me so I could check out the rhythmic movements of her ass while I thought about all the dirty things I would hopefully soon be doing to her. But she didn't know the way, so I was stuck up ahead. It was an easy hike in terms of terrain, but it would definitely take most of the morning. During the long expanses of silent trekking, I kept thinking about what was to come with great anticipation. What would she be like? Would she be shy, bold, wild, tender, passive? I figured that if it was her first time with a woman, she'd most likely be shy and tender, so that would probably be the best tone to take with her. I didn't want to scare her off.

I moved happily in the early morning light dappling the trees. It was chilly, and there was a fine mist in the air that felt pleasant on my skin. Even if Emma was scaring away the smaller creatures with her noisy plodding and occasional chattering, it was still a fine morning to traipse through the woods. This was where I felt most alive. And soon, I would share one of my favorite places with her. I breathed deeply and listened to birdsong while my mind wandered to the mysteries of this beautiful woman walking by my side in the deepest woods. I tried to imagine how she would climax. Would she spill over quietly? Would she clench and buck and swear? Would tears spill from her eyes as she clutched me close?

It was always such a thrill to discover new intimate territory. I had already glimpsed her shores, her valleys, peaks, and grasslands. Soon, I would explore and map them further. We both knew this expedition's ends went beyond navigating to the hot springs. There, we would navigate first contact with each other. Who would claim control? Would there be a struggle? If I planted my flag in her flesh, would she yield? She was a new world to me, and I wanted to know. Would she make me beg? Would I be the one to gasp at her touch? What sounds and movements, sensations and feelings awaited in our union? Such thoughts occupied my mind all the way to the spring.

We arrived before noon and stopped to eat. Emma made nervous small talk about the beauty of the spring. Canadian Shield rocks surrounded the spring, and steam rose off the two pools. The larger one was comfortably warm while the smaller pool's heat level was best for the brave.

"Let's do this," I announced, packing up the remains of our snack, then beginning to strip off my clothes with a sly expression.

She quickly turned away and asked, "So…do I just strip down to my bra and panties?" Her cheeks were burning. For some reason, her self-conscious uncertainty excited me.

"Nobody around here ever wears anything in the spring, but if that makes you uncomfortable, then I guess you can leave them on."

"Okay. Okay," she said. "Just don't look till I'm in, then. All right?"

My lips said, "All right," but my mind said, *I've already looked, and I intend to look long and hard before today is through.*

I turned and slipped into the warm water and felt an immediate rush of pleasure suffuse my body.

"You're not looking, right?" she asked too loudly.

I chuckled to myself and reassured her that I was looking away. I could hear her pad over to the spring's edge and dip a foot in.

"Oh, wow. That *is* really warm."

"The other pool is hotter, but you can't stay in it for long. This one is better for a good, lengthy soak. Are you in yet? Can I turn around?"

"Give me a second," she murmured and then slipped into the small pool. The knowledge that we were both naked and so close sent a shock of desire straight to my clit.

"Okay. You can turn around."

I turned to face her, and her exotic loveliness hit me all over again, like I was seeing her for the first time. She was breathtaking. Her hair, her gorgeous golden hair the color of sunshine, flowed freely down her shoulders and into the pool. And her eyes, her eyes were the softest spring sky blue. In this light, they seemed to have a faint purple tinge that made me think of chicory wildflowers, which brought such joyful pops of unusual color to any northern landscape. She didn't belong here. And yet here she was. Eyeing me shyly with flushed cheeks, hiding her chest with her folded arms. Here she was.

I had intended to seduce her with some witty banter before making a move. But she was so stunning, this pale stranger—naked, desiring, vulnerable—framed by the vast rugged backdrop of this northern terrain that I didn't dare sully the moment with shallow words. Amongst my people, silence is sacred. So I merely moved closer to her, holding her gaze. The air between us all but vibrated with longing, so I leaned in and kissed her.

Just Right

Kissing Win felt different. Different than I had expected kissing a woman to feel. Different than kissing a man. It wasn't too aggressive or too gentle. It was this incredible blend of both that made my flesh sing.

Above the water, the wind chilled my shoulders while below the water, our hands explored each other's curves. It was so strange and foreign and yet uncannily familiar to touch a woman like this. I slipped my hand down the curve of her back to the swell of her ass and cupped it. Nothing unusual there. But before me, her breasts bobbed in the water, inviting touch I did not yet dare. Her nipples were dark tan and squeezed tight. I wondered what they looked like when relaxed and how I might one day watch them respond to my touch, becoming crinkled and erect like this.

Win dared the touch I did not. She brought her mouth to my breast, kissing, sucking, and teasing with knowing skill. I ran my nails up and down her spine. I alternated between lightly trailing them until she shivered and firmly pressing them until they left my mark. Win moaned and brought her lips back to mine, her tongue seeming eager to explore my mouth. She pushed me against the rocks and moved against me, her curves mixing with mine in rhythmic time. I wrapped my legs about her waist, and we made waves in the little pool as our passion built.

"Come with me," she said with a growl, disentangling herself and making her way to the edge of the spring and our packs. She'd laid a giant blanket out by the spring and now held it out for me to wrap myself in.

"Where are we going?" I laughed, stumbling along as she took my hand and led me to a nearby grove of trees. Win ducked under a particularly huge coniferous tree with low-sweeping branches. I had no clue what kind of tree it was or what was going on, but I followed, giddy with lust. The tree's branches created a kind of shelter from the wind and cold, and it was needed, since even though it was around noon and the sun was at its peak, it was still a brisk autumn day. I was quickly cooling from the warmth of the spring. Win laid down a second blanket by the trunk and invited me to her. She was lying propped up on one elbow, winking and patting the ground beside her. It was weird and adorable, and I couldn't resist. I lay down next to her, propped up on one elbow too, and we snuggled under my blanket, giggling, kissing, and warming back up again.

Win grasped my breast boldly, eyebrow arched. I chuckled and grasped hers in answer. It was warm and soft yet firm. A shudder went through my body. Was I gay now? Was I just responding to the masculine parts of her? Was this just loneliness and experimentation at the end of days? I didn't know. But it felt right. I wanted her. Win began leisurely stroking and exploring my contours, holding my gaze with the gentlest of eyes. Every movement she made, I followed, mirroring her motions on her own flesh. She brushed the back of her hand against my inner thighs and I gasped. She smiled. I brushed the back of my hand against the soft fuzz of her inner thighs too. Her smile grew. She traced my hips, down my thighs, and then back up along the seam made by legs lying one on top of the other. She traced all the way up to my sex and lingered there a moment. I opened my legs for her, and her brilliant smile lit up our little makeshift shelter.

She began to gently explore my vulva as I slid my hand bravely between her thighs too. She was wet, and her lips felt like softest silk. My fingers glided over her lips and circled her clit. I could barely breathe for the thrill of it. This was what it was to touch a woman. I peered up joyfully at the sheltering strength of the tree. Win brought her mouth to mine, and I was lost in bottomless kisses. She touched me, and I touched her, and sensations blended and mingled us together until I couldn't tell who was who and what was what. I just knew that I wanted more. More of her. More. I wanted more.

Win came on top of me, pressing the full weight of her body onto me and gyrating rhythmically before kissing her way down my flesh to disappear beneath the blanket. I wasn't cold. I wanted to see. I pushed aside the blanket, and Win glanced up, a question clear in her eyes. I nodded, and she pushed apart my thighs and went down on me.

I had always preferred foreplay to intercourse because I never came except by focused attention to my clit, so Win's generous and experienced attention was more than appreciated. She knew her way around a pussy all right and lavished me with skilful concentration. It wasn't long at all before my climax washed over me like a wave crashing through me from the tips of my clenched toes to the crown of my head. I cried out and moaned in time with each contraction of pleasure, my hand wrapped in Win's braid and probably pulling far too tightly.

Win wiped her mouth with her hand and came up to kiss my lips. Her mouth still tasted like the most intimate part of me, and I liked it. I wanted to know her that way too.

"Let me return the favor," I whispered, my heart pounding wildly.

She moved from atop me and lay down, one knee raised, her hands laced behind her head. I looked at her tanned, toned, openly inviting body and swallowed my fear. I kissed my way down her torso, lingering in choice spot, before making my way to her mound. I hesitated here, uncertain. "I've never done this before."

"I know. You told me, remember?"

I blushed, remembering. And still I hesitated, unsure. Why was this so much scarier than going down on a guy? Was it because I was afraid of how much I'd like it?

"You don't have to," Win said. "I'd be happy to just make out and then love you some more later."

A crow landed on a tree branch far above our heads. It regarded us curiously, cawed, and then flew off.

"No, I want to. I really do," I murmured, nuzzling into the down between her thighs. Win parted her legs, and her warm, mildly spicy scent overcame the last of my hesitation. I slipped my tongue between her legs and tentatively flicked it over her clit. Her legs tensed, and I sensed a jolt of energy moving through her. It gave me confidence. I tried to copy the moves she and my previous lovers had performed on me, paying attention to not only her clit but to all of her velvety smooth vulva, changing up the sensations and building up the energy and rhythm. Judging by her breathing and the insistent way her hips were moving, I felt fairly confident that she was enjoying herself.

"I want your fingers inside me," Win said.

With a thrill of excitement, I slipped a finger gingerly inside Win's pussy and felt her shudder in response. I think I shuddered too. It felt incredible. So warm and tight and wet and wanting. I slipped in another and followed the urgent rhythm of Win's hips, driving her to a spectacular orgasm that gripped my fingers fiercely inside her as the spasms rocked my quivering hand. Her entire body shook, and she swore through clenched teeth as she came. I was in awe. How did I get here? Was this really happening?

Eventually, her muscles released me, and I slipped carefully from her sated pussy. I lay down beside her and tried to catch my breath and to not think too much about what all this meant.

"Shit, newbie. You've got skills."

We both laughed and snuggled awhile in contented silence, pulling the blanket back over us now that the heat of passion was dissipating. Despite my efforts not to overthink it, my mind was racing.

"I liked that," I said. "Sex with a woman is so sweet and tender. I think I really like it."

Win cackled. "Wrong on both counts, my dear."

"What? What do you mean?"

"I mean that I already explained that I'm not exactly a

woman. And I was only sweet and tender with you because it was your first time. If you want to try it rough, I'd be happy to oblige," she said, eyes a-twinkle.

"Oh, really?" I responded, putting flirty curiosity in every note.

"Yes, really. And you'd deserve it too," she added. "The way you strode into my place and just blatantly tried to take what's mine. Strutting around, trying to dazzle me with your shiny, yellow hair and your perky tits..." She twisted my nipple hard.

"Ow!" I said, a strange new buzz stirring within me. Win pulled on my nipples in a leisurely but harsh way. I wasn't sure I liked it. I wasn't sure I didn't.

"Come now, Emma. Didn't your mother ever teach you not to talk to strangers? There are dangers in the woods." She reached over, beyond my naked body, grabbed a small fallen branch, and started stripping parts off it as she spoke. "Somebody might tie you up. Somebody might make you sorry you strayed from the path."

I just looked at her, uncertainly.

She threw aside the blanket, exposing me to the elements and her hard gaze. "Lay on your stomach."

All I could hear was the blood whooshing in my ears. She was scaring me a little, and yet I felt my pussy get slick too. I obeyed and waited. She trailed the tree branch down the length of my back, over my bottom and all the way down to the soles of my feet. Then she brought it down swiftly on my ass. The needles pricked and smarted, and I jumped. Every part of me tingled with thoroughly alert excitement.

And that was when I knew. In precisely that odd, electrifying moment.

That was when I recognized that although the world I once knew might be in chaos, the authentic, natural world was still very much thriving. Win made me see it and even brought it out in me. I felt alive and vibrant in ways I never had before in my life. *This* was the world where I most truly belonged. Alongside this amazing human who reminded me of both my animality and my spirit.

Always before, I had been searching but never finding where I belonged. Always my partners were too this or too that. But Win and I fit.

S/he was just right.

PART THREE: BECOMING BRAVE
EMPOWERMENT EROTICA

SHY GIRL

I once worked as the towel girl at a sex club in Toronto. Go ahead and imagine what kind of girl takes a job like that. Do you imagine me a brazen, self-proclaimed slut, adorned in fishnets and heels? Maybe blond. Probably tattooed. Likely burdened with a traumatic past and some serious daddy issues. Yeah…that's not me. Though I met enough of those girls at the club to recognize the uneasy kernel of truth in the stereotype. I get it. I'm not the kind of girl you expect to find on the payroll of a swingers' association. A nice, university-educated, somewhat shy and quite a bit awkward girl from a good family just doesn't wind up in a place like that. Except that I did.

Blame my ex-husband. I certainly do. When I'm not blaming myself for every little thing I could have done wrong to make him leave. I tried so hard to do everything right. I really, truly tried to please him, to be a model wife, but he still left. Just turned to me, all blasé on a Tuesday night, and told me he was over it. It being the sacred vow we'd made before God and everyone who mattered in our lives. No big deal.

Craig was my high school sweetheart. The first and only man I'd ever slept with. When he left, I obsessively replayed virtually every interaction we'd ever had in our twelve years together, looking for clues to where I'd failed, despite everyone I knew repeatedly telling me it wasn't my fault.

My therapist. My friends. My cat, Mr. Snuggles. Okay, so he couldn't technically verbalize, but with every purr, I swear he was reinforcing the wisdom of my loved ones. I just couldn't figure out why my husband had left. I kept a beautiful home, I cooked well, I took care of all our social engagements and endlessly supported him emotionally. I watched every goddam sport he wanted, even though it bored me to tears, just because it made him happy to have me on the couch beside him while he ranted at the television.

The only area of our life where I felt that perhaps I hadn't exceled as a wife was the bedroom. How could I have known if I was good enough? I'd never been with anyone but him. I gave him a blowjob almost every day. I never said no. I tried everything he wanted to try. Okay, I drew the line at anything weird going up my butt, but anything at all going in and not out of that hole is weird as far as I'm concerned. Craig tried to show me all this anal porn, as if it would somehow convince me to try it when I saw other women enjoying ass play. But when I said I'd happily go along with it if we played "tit for tat," and I got to stick things up his ass too, he miraculously understood how a person could know that they wouldn't like something even if they hadn't tried it before. Funny that.

So even though I know it's a ludicrous reduction of an undoubtedly complex situation, I basically concluded that my ex-husband left because I refused to let him stick his dick in my asshole. Not because he himself was a dick and an asshole, which is much closer to the truth.

In a weird way, I learned a lot of truths at the sex club. Truths about human sexuality in general but mostly about my own body, identity, and desires. No one comes to the O Lounge looking for enlightenment, but you'd be surprised how often people find it. My friend, Zoe, doles it out alongside liquor at the bar. She was the one who got me the job. We'd been a bottle and a half of red wine into tear-filled, confessional bonding post-separation when she just threw it out there.

"You need to get laid. Well and often. By new people. That's how you get over a breakup. Multiple, mind-blowing orgasms with hot strangers. Come to the club with me sometime."

Zoe was my wild friend. I knew she was a bartender, but I'd assumed it was at a regular nightclub. That evening, over dangerously endless glasses of merlot, I learned the truth. And somehow, before I knew it, we wound up at the club, where Zoe took charge and loudly introduced me to people, dragging my drunken, shocked ass from room to room.

This place was like a portal to a whole other world, one I had never suspected existed. And I became someone I never knew existed. I carried on entire polite conversations with men sporting nothing but half-mast boners. I watched countless couples please each other sensually. I witnessed positions and kinks I had never considered before. With Zoe by my side, navigating the crowd and providing colorful commentary on the goings-on, I felt safe and protected to peek into this intriguing underworld of sexual freedom and excess. I remember that I kept laughing to myself, delighted at the sheer outlandishness of the entire situation, which was so out of character for someone as timid and white bread as me. Several men propositioned me that evening, but I denied them all, eager only to watch and learn. I felt like a stealth anthropologist, observing the mating habits of a foreign species. That already felt like such a huge step forward toward a more courageous and sexually liberated me. It was enough at that point.

The next morning, I woke with a horrendous hangover and a hazy sensation that it had all been a dream. Later that afternoon, when Zoe called to check in on me, she confirmed the reality and details of our evening. And reminded me that my first shift started at nine p.m. that night. I flipped the fuck out, and Zoe had quite the time talking me down, although I ultimately settled into the thought of making some extra spending money on the weekends just by handing out towels and sheets to perverts in the club's change-room. It seemed a simple enough gig and would give me more opportunities to observe other people exploring their sexuality, which I not so secretly enjoyed as a risk-free way to tiptoe up to exploring my own. So that was how it began. The strangest job I'd ever had.

The first week was thrilling. I enjoyed watching people, observing their diversity of looks and attitude. Some were confident, others nervous, a few were clearly ashamed, but many were simply on the prowl. There was every race, body type, age, and walk of life represented. I found it fascinating. I made up stories in my head about the strangers I saw. In the couple's play area, there was a middle-aged long-term couple, looking to spice up their love life by showing off their impressive sexual skills for others' viewing pleasure. A safe, exhibitionist form of naughtiness that clearly excited them both and brought them closer. In the next room, a much older woman with piercings and purple hair was howling her pleasure while being gangbanged by men half her age. Maybe she was a widow. Maybe she had watched her friends die, one by one, and wanted to live it up and fulfill all her fantasies before she too lay cold in the ground, the sweet pleasure of her flesh wasting away. And behind the glory hole in the wall kneeled a trans woman, eagerly pleasing strangers with her mouth. What had she lived through to get here? What price had she paid to live her truth? I could only imagine.

Her pleasure brought me joy, as all of theirs did. But I never joined in the pleasure. I never sought my own. I just did the laundry, watched, and fantasized. I facilitated their adventures and demurred whenever someone invited me into the fun. Which wasn't very often. And not just because I was on staff and working. I knew how to make myself invisible. I was a mousy brunette, and I didn't even dress up much for my shifts, unlike the other staff, who used the opportunity to indulge in the pleasure of parading around in outrageously slutty outfits. I just wanted to be invisible. The proverbial fly on the wall. Observing but not observed. That felt safest while I figured out what I wanted, which must have been to discover what I had done wrong in my conjugal relations with Craig and how to keep the next man I loved. At least, that was what I figured at first.

By the end of the first month, I had already become somewhat blasé about the club. "Another day, another orgy," I'd joke with Zoe when we'd start our shifts. I'd settled into a somewhat comfortable routine there, even if sometimes I went home after a shift, masturbated furiously, then burst into inexplicable tears. It was hard to get what I wanted when I didn't really know what that was. And so the first month working at the club, I merely observed, trying to find clues to some mysterious lack in myself that I figured must be responsible for the failure of my marriage. I didn't actually know what I wanted beyond that. And I had never truly considered the possibility that there was nothing wrong with me at all.

Enter the dominatrix.

I feel she needs a dramatic introduction in this story, for she certainly was one in my life. Everything changed for me after I met her. There was me before, and there was me after, and those two women are very different people.

I was walking across the salon, the area of the club where people hang out to drink and socialize before changing to engage in play. I was carrying a load of fresh laundry to fold in the locker room when my attention was drawn to a lively conversation on one of the couches. She was there, holding court, charming lookers-on with some entertaining anecdote while sipping a martini and permitting a hooded slave to massage her feet. She was stunning. Asian, with black hair that was shaved on one side and fashioned into classy, 1920s-style finger waves that reached just to her chin on the other side. She was clad entirely in form-fitting latex, her every curve on display in a ruffled ivory blouse and black pencil skirt. Impossibly high heels sat tidily arranged by her side, no doubt carefully removed by her faceless submissive so that he could knead her feet.

Her gaze happened upon me, and I realized with a start of horror that my mouth was actually hanging open like I was some kind of ridiculous fool, so I jerked forward. Then stumbled on someone's wayward handbag, spilling the laundry all over the floor. Mortified, I rushed to throw it all back into the basket and make a hasty exit.

Her peal of tinkling laughter haunted me as I scurried to the relative obscurity of the change-room, where I struggled to calm my madly beating heart. I noticed that my hands were trembling as I tried to fold the towels. What the hell was wrong with me? I wondered, simultaneously wondering about a zillion things concerning that woman and her slave, who they were, and how they expressed their sexuality. I shook a sheet out forcefully and began folding it into a neat package, the actions soothing my mind and slowing my heart's frantic beating, as though putting the linens in order was putting my thoughts in order too.

When I looked up, she was standing before me, a foot from my face, and I shrieked and jumped off the ground. She laughed again, and my heart thrilled at the sound and the way her features lit up with joy. Sweat broke out on my body, and I didn't know what to do with my eyes or my hands. I grabbed a towel and shoved it clumsily toward her. She didn't take it. She just let it waver there in the space between us. I didn't know what to do. I slowly, awkwardly let it fall.

"You're new," she said, and her voice was velvety with amusement. "What's your name?"

I squeaked out a reply in a nervous voice that hardly sounded like my own. I couldn't even look at her; she was too beautiful. Too much.

"And what's a shy little mouse like you doing in a place like this?"

"I…I'm the towel girl," I mumbled lamely.

"I can see that. I'd like to see you, though. Look at me when I speak to you." She reached out a finger to gently lift my chin and coax my gaze to meet hers. Her eyes were deepest brown. Her expression sensual, patient, and accepting. "Why are you here? What are you looking for?"

My mind reeled. What could I say to this gorgeous, exacting stranger? Her bearing would permit no less than raw honesty, and my eyes welled up. Through the veil of my tears, her expression did not change, and somehow, I knew that whatever I had to say, this woman could hold it.

It came out in an anxious, breathy rush. Everything about Craig. My failing and uncertainty. My curiosity. Even though it was an inappropriate over-share, it felt right. Her gaze continued to hold mine. She waited and listened attentively, as though nothing else existed or mattered beyond this moment of confession between us, two strangers in a seedy underworld of illicit longing. And I longed for her. To know me. To touch me. I risked telling her what I knew. "So…I was always a good girl and now…I…I don't want to be anymore." Still, she waited. Like she knew that I wasn't done. I searched around inside myself and found something that still needed to be said. "But…I guess I'm scared. I just watch other people. I haven't been sure yet, and I want to be sure."

She nodded slowly. "That was brave of you to share, little mouse." An odd thrill went through me at her use of a pet name. She reached out and carefully, silently, loosed my hair from its untidy ponytail, arranging it about my face and assessing the effect coolly. I couldn't breathe. I was kicking myself for not trying to look nice. She was so polished and stylish. Did she find me pretty? Did I please her?

At last, she broke the silence between us, asking, "Do

you think you might enjoy having my help in becoming a bad girl?"

Heat rushed through my entire body, and I struggled to voice a simple, enthusiastic yes. Oh. My. God. Yes.

She nodded slowly again. "I like my playthings to address me as Mistress X. Can you do that?" It was my turn to nod. "Excellent. And will you be a good little mouse and trust me enough to give up control tonight?" More nodding on my part. "Okay. You can always let me know if you're not sure about something by saying 'yellow.' And if you definitely don't like something, you just have to say 'red.' All right?"

She came closer then. Close enough that I was torturously aware of the proximity of her lips, painted enticingly scarlet. "Now, is there anything in particular that you do or do not want tonight?" Her breath was warm and smelled delicious. She moved her mouth close to my ear. "You can whisper it to me, little mouse." She kissed my earlobe gently, then took it between her teeth and nibbled. My knees buckled a bit, and I struggled to think. "What do you want?" she whispered, and the sound of her breathing, the scent of her body pressed close to me made my mind swirl. I didn't think. I just answered without even really knowing what I was saying.

"I want your hands on me. Your...fingers inside me. I want everyone to see."

"You want me to fuck you in front of everyone, my pet?" she said, making eye contact with me. My cheeks burning with embarrassment and excitement, I nodded once again, not trusting myself to speak.

"All right. Follow me," she said, beginning to walk away, her ass a veritable piece of art in her skin-tight skirt. That was when I had the horrifying realization that I was supposed to be working. A choked little gasp escaped my throat, and she turned to see what was wrong. My face must have betrayed my tormented thoughts, for she laughed again and reassured me. "I know your boss, Fernando. He won't mind me putting on a show with the towel girl." She reached out her hand with the most beguiling smile. "Trust me," she said, and I obeyed, taking her hand and following her into the library.

I'd always found this room to be weirdly named, since there were no books in the library. Only BDSM equipment and a seating area for voyeurs. Her slave was kneeling in a corner, presumably waiting for her. A thrill of excitement seemed to run through his body at her return, like he had purpose and meaning once more. She resolutely ignored him, though, and steered me to the center of the room where she boldly took charge. "How many of you got a towel from this sweet young thing?" she asked loudly. Some of the assembled raised their hands. "And how many of you would like to see me fuck this sweet young thing?" All hands in the room raised, save those stopped by restraints.

I could feel my cheeks burning hot with both fear and excitement. I'd never been with a woman. I'd never engaged in any kind of BDSM play. I'd never sought attention like this. It was all really new and utterly electrifying.

Mistress X moved behind me and began to feel me up, tracing her hands teasingly along my contours. She played to the crowd. "This one's shy, everyone. She needs encouragement. Make some noise if you'd like to see what she's hiding behind these boring work clothes." The crowd roared, and Mistress sensually stripped me of my shirt, throwing it dramatically into the seating area, where it was caught by an older gentleman wearing a leather chest harness and a gigantic smile.

She addressed her slave then. "Minion, you'll fetch her clothes and keep them nice and tidy for her to put back on when we're through. Understood?" The slave nodded and eagerly set to his task as Mistress X began trailing manicured nails along the swell of cleavage peeking above the cups of my everyday cotton bra. I wished I'd worn something more exciting, but the bra and panties were a new baby-blue set that was comfortable and cute, if not exactly typical sex club attire. She flicked a strap down one shoulder, and a woman on the couch began to shout encouragement. Others joined in. Next thing I knew, my bra was unclasped and falling to the floor to great, rowdy fanfare, and Mistress X's hands were on me, cupping my tits as the bra once had. Her hands were warm and gentle but firm, and she held me tight in the spotlight, whispering in my ear, "Relax, my pet. Your only job is to enjoy. Do you trust me?"

I nodded, closed my eyes, and leaned back into her strength, drawing from it. I couldn't help but smile. Who was this girl? With her tits out in front of total strangers? She was someone brave and sexy and confident. I decided I liked her. I wiggled out of my pants and thong with Mistress's help, and she paraded me around the room for a bit, showing off what I usually sought to hide. "Look how pretty she is beneath all those layers," she cooed. "We've got a stealth hottie on our hands tonight, everybody."

I blushed and blushed as she toured me around for the appraisal of others until she mused aloud, "Look at her blush. She's so cute and shy. I wonder if I can get her other cheeks just as red as these ones with a little spanking." This musing was met with wild applause, and I was steered toward her slave, who assumed a position on all fours. Mistress X sat on him as though he were a human bench, then beckoned me to position myself across her lap. She looked so regal and powerful, I dared not hesitate but poured myself into the form of her pleasure, feeling vulnerable, exposed, and aroused.

People crowded close, and I felt their eyes on me. Felt myself the object of their desire for once. But mostly, I felt her. A strong, feminine, and commanding force directing me. She traced her nails up the backs of my thighs to my ass, lightly at first and then with increasing pressure. It began to border on the edge of pain, and I wondered if it would leave a mark. I weirdly hoped that it would. That I could hold on to the wounds as some of kind of visual proof that this crazy experience really did happen. I wanted her to mark me as hers. I wanted to belong to her. To be special and chosen. And it was all new. These odd, novel thoughts and wants. I'd never felt anything like this before. I hardly recognized myself, but I didn't worry about it, because there was no space to do so. I was so caught up in reveling in the thrill of these new feelings. Mistress X began to knead my ass cheeks, and I felt my sex grow slick at the sensation, then slicker still at the thought that all these strangers were watching me grow wet. A pretty woman began to play with her nipples as she stared. Her partner stroked his cock lightly as his eyes too never left the sight of me, yielding under Mistress's elegant, capable hands.

She spanked me. In an unpredictable rhythm that left me guessing and trembling with anticipation. At turns lulling, then startling. Deceptively gentle, then fierce. And she talked the whole time, her voice accompanying the slaps with maddening taunts and compliments, provocations and invitations. I wanted her so badly. I wanted her fingers to slip inside me and fuck me ferociously until I couldn't remember who or where I was. I begged. I moaned. I pleaded. But still she said she wouldn't give me what I wanted until I was ready.

"I'm ready, I'm ready," I implored. But she was unconvinced.

"I think you can want me more. I think you could be wetter. What do you think, Joe?" she asked, addressing a random person in the crowd.

"She's pretty damn wet," Joe said.

"Fuck her already," urged the pretty woman with her fingers twisting her nipples. Her handsome partner nodded, picking up the pace, stroking his cock.

"You think you're ready, mouse?" Mistress purred, delivering three particularly powerful whacks to my already red and imprinted bottom.

I growled a fierce "Yes," and she laughed and released me.

"Stand up. Minion will prepare you."

I stood on shaking legs as Minion rushed to affix me to the giant wooden St. Andrews cross in the room. I was too dazed with desire to even wonder how he knew what she wanted and meant. The wood felt sturdy and solid beneath me, like my bindings once they held me fast. My legs were spread apart in a forced position of exposure that heightened my already riotous lust. I wanted her. I needed her. Right now. Had I known yearning before this moment? Trembling, I watched as Minion fetched a black latex glove that she carefully fitted to her right hand while holding searing eye contact with me the entire time. She sauntered close, pressed her body toward mine. I could hear the odd, rubbery squeak of her latex dress moving against her curves with every slight movement of her flesh. I could feel her heat and the building pressure of my own ravenous want of her.

She surprised me with a kiss. A sweet, taunting, tempting kiss. It was unexpected because I wasn't sure she'd deign to kiss her playthings. That kind of tenderness wasn't what I'd seen happening as part of this room's dynamics on previous evenings. Most interactions in the library focused on pain and power. But the moment her lips met mine, I wanted more. More. I strained against my restraints to feel her again, but she moved just out of reach and smiled. She watched my mounting desperation with bemused detachment, and I realized where power came in here too. An odd flash of anger leapt up in me, and I all but growled, straining against my ties. But she only laughed again, that lovely throaty laugh, before leaning in close once more and allowing my lips to find hers. Oh my God, her lips…they were soft and sweet and delectable, and I couldn't get enough.

Our tongues danced inside each other's mouths before she broke away to whisper in my ear, "You want me to fuck you in front of all these people, don't you?"

I do. I do. My knees threatened to give way with the sheer, outlandish craving of it.

"Let's show them how beautiful you are. How sexy." And she began to kiss, lick, and nibble her way down my flesh. I strained at my bindings again. Tippy-toed. Wriggled closer. Sank back. I writhed in my tiny allowable orbit as she tormented me beyond what I thought I could take, murmuring suggestive phrases all the while.

And then her hand was on me. Between my legs. At last. Expertly parting my lips and teasing about my clit. My entire body shook with the immensity of a great desire at the breaking point. I had no shame. I begged her to fuck me—and finally, finally—she did. Slipping powerfully inside me and skillfully pumping away at me. Filling me with her graceful, strong fingers. At last, at last, giving me exactly what I finally knew I wanted. I felt an overwhelming sensation swell like a fucking tsunami wave within me, rising and rising in power until my pussy exploded intensely on her hand, and I was squirting wildly all over the place to much enthusiastic applause, thinking only of her, only and always of her, Mistress X.

What a beautiful memory. I recall my shock at ejaculating for the first time. I remember the older gentleman quietly achieving orgasm at the same moment, his eyes only leaving mine to close in the throes of his own ecstasy. I'll never forget the look of abject jealousy in Minion's eyes, but I also distinctly remember realizing that Zoe was there, hooting loud and raucous encouragement for my long-awaited erotic escapade.

Mistress was pleased. She patted my hair and called me her "brave little mouse," an epithet that sent a shiver of pure satisfaction right through me. And I realized with wonder that it pleased me most of all to please her. So I went on pleasing her and being pleased by her until this shy little mouse finally learned how to roar with the best of them. Because one of the truths that I learned while working at that sex club is that sometimes shy girls just need a little encouragement, and the right touch, to be the wildest girls of all.

TOUGH AS NAILS

I wouldn't say I had a crush on Thuy. It wasn't the dictionary definition of a brief but intense infatuation with someone unattainable or inappropriate. Well, not exactly. Sure, it was intense, and I was enthralled, but a crush implied that I understood and obsessively wallowed in the impossibility of the attraction. It didn't explain the undercurrent of horror that initially flowed through me alongside the enchantment whenever she looked at me. Although I suppose the word in its original verb form captured that. The pressure, the fear of being violently subdued, of being inalterably transformed. I was, on some level, afraid of being crushed. There was definitely that. How could there not be? Thuy was everything I was afraid to be. She was like a loud and proud manifestation of my secrets. She was terrifying. And sexy. Secrets definitely have sex appeal.

Driving to the little theatre where her dance troupe was performing, I felt both dread and excitement intermingling in my body in a confusing maelstrom of emotion. I kept obsessively checking out my fingernails, which were painted fiery red, a color I would never have chosen for myself, but one that Thuy had chosen for me. She chose this shade, and I let her. I gave myself over to her in this, and she gave me crimson. At the time, I didn't understand the profundity of the gift. For that night, we painted more than my nails red.

We painted the evening red. And I was transformed, just as I had feared. Though I liked the new shape I assumed under the force of Thuy's charismatic touch.

We met at the salon. She was my manicurist, working there part-time to pay the bills as she pursued her passion for dance. She was mixed-race, Vietnamese and Caucasian, which she spoke of openly in a refreshing way that was so different from my own approach to my mixed-race heritage. She didn't have to tell everyone; she could have passed as white, like me. But she loved to tell stories of her mom, a feisty, hardworking immigrant who owned the only nail salon in a small Canadian town. I'd grown up in a small town too. One rife with racism, so in my family, we never talked about the indigenous roots that were part of our family tree. I'd always grown up sensing it was something private that other people didn't need to know about. So when I moved to this large university city and met other people who claimed their diverse racial identities with pride, it made me uncomfortable. Like seeing lesbians who made their identity so obvious. Their visibility scared me. I was in something faintly resembling and yet distinct from a closet. Perhaps something like an armoire. I mean, I wasn't exactly hiding my sexuality, but I also didn't advertise it. Or I didn't think I did, and yet somehow, Thuy had known that it was okay to flirt with me. When I'd questioned her about it, she'd laughed and pronounced, "Straight girls don't keep their nails this short."

Thuy. I loved her name. When she told me, I'd imagined it spelled like it sounded: Twee. I'd laughed, then had to explain. "Sorry, it's just that 'twee' means 'overly cute,' and there's nothing cute about you." She'd raised an eyebrow, and I'd realized my mistake, stumbling over my words, rushing to explain what I really meant, how she was strong and bold and anything but saccharine. She wasn't offended, though. If anything, she'd seemed amused by my mortification at accidentally insulting her.

"It's okay. My name doesn't fit in Vietnamese either. Thuy means gentle woman. My poor mother was so off base. She should have called me Long. It means dragon." She'd winked at me here, and my heart had clenched, for I'd loved the way her eyes twinkled whenever she was toying with me.

"Our names mean pretty much the same thing," I'd replied. "Sarah means lady."

"Ha! Seems like your mom hit the nail on the head with that one."

She'd proceeded to tease me some more about the fact that I never got anything but a French manicure. She thought it was boring to get the same look over and over again when there was such an abundance of choice. Her own nails were always stunning, full of innovative designs and fun colors. But I liked how classy and clean the French manicures made my hands look, with just that little tip of white over a pink-tinged base. It was like my real nails, but with a beauty filter applied. The crispness of the airbrushed white line satisfied me. It reminded me of a smart little sailor cap or fresh linens on a clothesline. There was something orderly and cute about it. Like an old-fashioned nurse's uniform. Every single time I showed up at the salon, she'd try to convince me to try something new. It became a running joke with all her coworkers, who started to call me Frenchie. "Thuy, Frenchie's here for her usual."

When I'd pay, Thuy would pester me playfully, "I don't want a tip, Sarah. I just want you to branch out a bit. Let me pick the color next time," to which I'd always reply, "Maybe," with absolutely no intention of doing so.

But the more I went to the salon and the more we talked, the closer we became, and the more I felt curious to know what it would be like to give myself over to this woman, who was clearly interested in me and flirting with me. The way she held my hands as she deftly applied the polish. The way her eyes held me with something amused and inviting. The pleasure I'd feel when she'd massage scented lotion onto my hands and forearms at the end of the manicure. It was all becoming more than impersonal. In fact, it had become positively fraught with unstated and simmering temptation. I'd started to overthink my outfit each time I went. I began to plan interesting things to talk to her about. That was when I finally broke and promised to let her choose my polish color next time.

She made a big deal about it with her coworkers, who'd chimed in with suggestions. I booked the appointment, drove home, and promptly masturbated with a ferocity that seemed out of proportion to the import of the appointment, which was not a date, after all. Though perhaps my body knew something that my mind didn't yet.

When I showed up for the appointment, the whole salon was in on it. Thuy had a way of bringing everyone together to share in any joy, and this silly moment was no exception. Her coworkers made a fuss at my arrival, and the other clients looked at me curiously as they clucked around me. I was embarrassed but also oddly exhilarated by the attention. I wasn't ever one to stand out, but I certainly did that day, especially once Thuy arrived with a blindfold, which she insisted on me wearing so that her big reveal of the final results of the manicure would not be ruined.

It felt weird and thrilling to be bereft of vision, surrounded by so many women's curiosity and attention as Thuy guided me to the chair and began her magic. I could feel my cheeks burning, and I had to force myself to breathe normally, to try to slow down my heartbeat as it raced excitedly. Thuy was silent the entire time, but the clients and coworkers never stopped commenting during the entire process. It felt strange to yield to the unknown under so much observation. My mind swirled with questions, and my body felt charged up, like I was almost vibrating with energy. I felt Thuy's touch as never before. I really noticed the focused skill with which she worked, her touch light and practiced, as she nudged my hands to follow her will. For the first time, I allowed myself to really feel how much I was attracted to her. To recognize how I was drawn to her and to acknowledge all the little things I found enticing. Like how much I loved the way her dark hair framed her delicate features. The way her easy smiles lit up her entire face with a kind of impish joy. The way she moved through the everyday world with a dancer's innate grace. By the time she was finishing up, massaging moisturizer into my hands, lacing her fingers through mine, I was breathless and wet with desire.

The big reveal happened to much collective oohing and aahing. But Thuy remained uncharacteristically silent, watching my face intently as I reacted to the bold color choice and spluttered my thanks. She refused to take my money, saying this one was on her. She handed me a piece of paper.

"Come to my show tonight."

Heat flushed through my entire body at the thought of seeing her dance, and I struggled to form a coherent response, so I simply nodded, feeling overwhelmed.

She took my hands in hers, ostensibly to look at her work, although I felt the promise pulsing beneath the gesture. "Wear something to match your manicure," she suggested obscurely before letting my hands go.

I must have tried on two dozen outfits before settling on this one, which bore exactly zero relation to my manicure, whatever the hell that even meant. But I felt good in it. Sleek black pants with a fitted white blouse. Heels. A hint of lace visible beneath the open buttons at my décolletage. Every bit the lady. Excepting the vulgar red polish, which I felt awkward sporting. Admittedly, it was an exciting color. Every time I saw my fingernails, I thought of stop signs and sex and death and passion. I kept trying to hide my hands in my pockets because it felt too brash, too unlike me. And yet, I also sort of loved it, loved how Thuy had left her mark on me, how I now wore a symbol of the parts of her that I most admired.

I had no idea what to expect of the show. The advertisement she had handed me said that her dance troupe, Brazen Moon, was belly dance meets tribal fusion. I should have known from the audience members that I was out of my element. I had never been surrounded by so many tattooed, pierced, and dreaded individuals in my life.

But the lights went down, the music started, and I forgot my discomfort in that crowd as I lost myself in the mesmerizing beauty onstage. The show was a kind of revelation. I never knew that anything like this existed. Women of all different races, ages, and sizes moved across the stage space with such unique style and flair. A woman who must have been in her sixties belly-danced with endearing coquettishness, revealing skin softened by time but no less sensually appealing. A group of lively gothic pirates roused the audience with playful choreography and an impressive use of handheld fans. The fans had long swaths of blue fabric made to resemble ocean waves. Then there was a memorable trio of what I can only describe as demented nurses, whose performance completely freaked me out as they jerked zombie-style across the stage with pantyhose over their faces, disfiguring their features. I was transfixed by their movements but honestly relieved when their time was over.

Then came Thuy, who I almost didn't recognize. She had little horns and was carrying a skull. She was clad all in black, some parts sheer, some torn, some leather, some buckled, all of it coming together with her makeup and accessories to suggest some kind of teeny demoness. The music was otherworldly and spectacular, as was her performance. She moved with sprightly grace, undulating across the stage with incredible muscle control, moving her tiny chest and the taut expanse of her belly with great precision in varied, shifting directions. She never once smiled, which was so unlike her that I questioned whether it was really her. But I recognized her tattoos. That dark imp was definitely Thuy, only a Thuy transformed into some fiendish sprite I didn't know and wasn't sure I wanted to, even as I was totally sure I wanted to. It was like she manifested exactly what I felt most compelling and repelling about her in that wicked character. I was captivated.

After the show, she found me while flushed with excitement, a sheen of sweat glistening on her flesh. "Can you wait for me? I've got to lock up tonight, but if you just hang out here, maybe we could spend some time together after?"

I was enthralled after that performance, so I would have agreed to anything she suggested. And I did. Oh, how I did.

It started off innocently enough: the only two left all alone in an empty theatre when Thuy suggested that she continue making me over. She bid me try on random bits of costumes hanging on racks scattered here and there in the green room. She tried to show me a few simple belly dance moves. She had some liquor with her. We drank and laughed and played dress-up like little girls. Except the feelings coursing through me were anything but innocent.

We found a bright red crinoline skirt in a closet, and Thuy just about lost her mind with excitement. "It's perfect! You have to wear it. It matches your nails."

I realized that perhaps that was what she'd meant. That I should wear something exuberant, attention-grabbing, flirty, and feminine like this flouncy skirt of ruffled suggestiveness. Everything else that I'd tried on that evening had gone on over my clothes, but something was shifting between us. I could feel the whiskey melting my boundaries. Or maybe it was the magic of this space, where I could be anything I wanted to be. I wasn't sure. But I knew I wanted to wear this brazenly sensual thing for her. That I wanted her to see me that way.

Still, I felt shy. This wasn't like me. The desire to be seen and the desire to hide fought for dominance within me until I finally asked her to turn around. She did, and I took off my heels and pants, then slipped the frilly skirt up my legs and over my hips. The moment I did so, my hips had to twist, twirling the frills this way and that. Irrepressible laughter spilled from my lips, and Thuy turned round.

"Yes," she said simply, nodding. I stood, trusting, in the heat of her gaze and silently willed her to make a move. She must have read my mind because she stepped closer, close enough for me to wriggle under the anticipation of her touch, and said, "I think what's under this blouse will go better with the crinoline." She looked at me for a signal of consent, and when I inclined my head, she began unbuttoning my blouse, her fingers brushing my chest with maddening focus. The blouse, with its crisp, ironed formality, fell to the floor, leaving behind only a silky white camisole edged with lace.

She kissed me, her mouth warm and sensual on mine. She tasted faintly of maple, the sweet flavoring of the whiskey we had drunk. But more than that, she tasted of freedom, a taste I didn't even realize I was yearning for.

She grabbed my shoulders and slowly twirled me around until I was facing the mirror at the dressing table, one of those stereotypical theatre ones with the lightbulbs all along the frame.

"Stay here. Don't move."

She moved away, and I was left feeling anxious, embarrassed to look at myself in the mirror.

She flicked on the mirror lights and turned off the harsh overhead ones. It was such a simple change in lighting, but it had a magical effect in the room. I felt rather than saw her return to me, her body pressed against me from behind.

"Look at you," she whispered in my ear before nibbling on my earlobe and kissing her way down my neck as her hands explored my curves.

So I did look. And it was strange and uncanny to see someone I hardly recognized in the mirror. A siren being courted by a demoness. It made me smile. It made my hips move in time with Thuy's. I closed my eyes to better take in the sensation of moving with her in this sensual dance of sorts. Her mouth and hands traced patterns of longing on me, and I all but melted beneath them.

Our eyes kept returning to the mirror. Her hand slipped beneath my crinoline, and I moaned, leaning back against her. She was small but strong. A force to be reckoned with. She could hold her own and hold me too. Her hand kept creeping higher, higher, toward my sweet spot as we undulated together in the mirror's illumination. Her eyes kept asking, and my whimpers kept answering. At last, her fingers reached their goal and flicked across my clit over my soaking wet panties. My whole body trembled in response, and Thuy flashed a wicked grin. She showed me just what a devil she could be, teasing me mercilessly over my underwear until I was trembling and begging her.

When her fingers slipped inside me, it was like a jolt of electricity passed through my entire body, and I almost buckled, but she held me fast. She held me tight and close and finger-fucked me furiously to the edge of orgasm. I wanted to come so badly, but I always reached this excruciating point where my body wouldn't let me. Not when I was with a partner. On my own, I could achieve relatively quick and satisfying orgasms, but somehow with a partner, everything felt more intense, and I would always shut down right when I was most likely to spill over the edge and lose control. Seeing myself in the mirror wasn't helping at this point, and I started to protest and push Thuy away.

"Sorry. Sorry. I can't. Not like this."

Though I worried I was ruining everything, Thuy was nonplussed. "Okay, what's wrong? What do you need?" she asked, her breath coming fast.

I struggled to find the words to say, but Thuy tried to help.

"Do we need a scene change? Here, come with me." She grabbed my hand, hers still sticky with my juices, and pulled me from the green room. She led me to the stage where all the women had been dancing earlier tonight. She placed me directly centre stage, kissed my forehead, and said once more, "Stay here. Don't move."

She left to fiddle with lights, but this time, I felt more comfortable waiting, knowing a distance between us had been bridged. Who would we be on this stage? What would we do? I looked around at the empty seats and imagined them filled with people eager to watch a different kind of performance. I was shocked to feel my thighs get slick with desire at the thought. I was anything but an exhibitionist. But then again, there wasn't really anyone here. And I wasn't myself tonight. I was...Scarlet. And she was brave and strong and sexy.

The lights kept changing. When they took on a look I liked, I yelled out, "That's it. Now get over here," in a bossy tone that was entirely unladylike.

Thuy skipped back to me, and our bodies met again in an eager embrace.

"I want to ride your face in front of all these imaginary people," I said, gesturing to the empty chairs.

Thuy visibly started with surprise and delight, then dramatically fell to the stage floor with a "Fuck yeah!"

I stood towering over Thuy and boldly straddled her face. I began swinging my crinoline flirtatiously back and forth like a Moulin Rouge cancan dancer. I flashed the audience and Thuy and just thoroughly enjoyed being outrageously sexual.

"Come closer," Thuy growled impatiently, and I obeyed, bringing my sex gingerly to her face, arranging my skirts about her.

The moment her tongue first touched me was electrifying, just like the first moment her fingers had. I peeled the camisole from my torso and flung it dramatically away, to much imaginary hooting and hollering. I reached behind my back for the clasps of my bra and imagined the breathless anticipation of my fictional spectators. I unhooked the clasps and set my breasts free to dance in time to my hips' movement, responding to the cadence of Thuy's skilled tongue. I danced here a time before gathering up my skirts to check in on Thuy. "You okay down there? Can you breathe?"

"Forget about me. Just come all over my face, beautiful."

How could I turn down such a compelling invitation? Though I'd never come with a partner before, I felt the first stirrings of possibility that perhaps this time, I could. Thuy couldn't see my face, and I couldn't see hers, and yet I felt seen and sexy in a way I never had before. I felt safe. And daring. I realized that sometimes playing a character allowed me to be more myself than I'd ever been before. So I gathered my breasts in freshly manicured hands and I belly-danced on this gorgeous, funny, brave woman's face to a spectacular orgasm, one that left me gasping for air and crying. But I took my pleasure and took it loudly, unapologetically filling the space with the song of my bliss.

How strange that I couldn't watch myself orgasm, and I couldn't let a partner watch me orgasm, but somehow, the thought of this imaginary audience doing so pushed me over the precipice of my own inhibition. I couldn't explain it. And I didn't have to. Thuy just held me while I shook through the fading waves of emotional and physical intensity.

Scarlet might have been make-believe, but she made me believe in a part of me that needed some faith and some coaxing to come out and play. In that little theatre, on that empty stage, Thuy and I played out our fantasies. Secrets were given space. Hunger was given the spotlight. I had always been somewhat repressed in my desire and rather dainty in my lovemaking, but when I finger-fucked Thuy to her own spectacular orgasm that night, there was nothing dainty or repressed about the way my ruby-tipped fingers darted in and out of her pussy. If there had been real spectators in the front row, they would have endured a splashing reminiscent of the front row for the killer whale show at Marineland, for Thuy ejaculated powerfully under my decidedly coarse and unrefined finger-blasting.

Tangled up on that stage, holding hands, struggling to catch our breath under those blinding lights, I realized I could be mixed in more ways than one. That it wasn't always either or. That I could be strong *and* soft. Classy *and* sexual. White *and* indigenous. Shy *and* bold. Feminine *and* gay. All the things that people tried to tell me didn't belong together. Even as they said that opposites attract.

Five years later, Thuy and I are still together, still loving the complexity of each other in all our differences and similarities. Five years later, this thing between us remains strong and tender.

Together, we are crushing it.

O Come, All Ye Faithful

I've always loved Christmas. The lights, the presents, the baked goods, the time with friends and family, I love it all. I know there are Grinches out there who "bah humbug" the season as an orgy of gross overconsumption, but for me, there has always been something magical about it that I never outgrew. It probably helps that gift-giving is my number one love language, my preferred way to provide and receive love. Finding the perfect gift for someone I care about is like my secret mission from the moment we meet. I'm always listening for little hints about things, big and small, that will bring a smile to their lips and a twinkle to their eye. It gives me a precious little thrill to stumble upon the perfect thing or to suss out a secret desire from someone I want to please. I'm definitely a pleaser, which has both its blessings and its burdens. But I truly love caring for people and making their lives easier. It genuinely brings me joy.

Which is why breakups are so hard for pleasers like me. There is no one sadder than a caretaker with no one to take care of. Especially if said caretaker was unceremoniously dumped via text a week before Christmas. I still can't believe how cold Tara turned out to be. Who does that? Especially right now, in the midst of pandemic lockdown? As a single person, I'm allowed to bubble with one other household through the holidays, despite the lockdown orders, and I thought Tara would be that household.

Now Christmas is tomorrow, and I have no plans to see anyone. Why bother, really? I'm too miserable to be around other humans anyway, and I already told my parents that I'd be bubbling with Tara. I also already bought her Christmas presents. All neatly wrapped and currently sitting in my closet as a haunting reminder, like the Ghost of Christmas That Never Was. What am I supposed to do with myself now? I've already cried for hours, scrolled through our old photos and texts, drunk too much wine, eaten several chocolate bars, and listened to all the saddest Christmas carols on repeat, every classic about being alone for the holidays. What is left for me to do to fill this terrible time?

But then I get an idea. An awesome idea. I get a wonderful, awesome idea.

I jump in my car and make for the local sex shop, the one with the really creative window displays. I came here with Tara a few weeks ago, and we spent a good half hour just browsing through the wares and laughing together, feeling connected and naughty. We didn't really buy anything except for some incense that the store was randomly selling alongside its predictable inventory of bongs and dongs. Neither of us are particularly into sex toys. It was just a spontaneous impulse to look around.

But now I am on a mission. I have been saving up some money, hoping to surprise Tara with a romantic getaway once all this COVID bullshit is over. But there's no use holding on to the money now. Who knows when it will be safe to travel again? What I do know is that my pussy could use some Christmas spirit, so why not blow it all, right here and now, on every single sex toy that catches my eye? Every one we looked at curiously together. I deserve my holly jolly Christmas, and I am going to get it, one way or another. This year, it will be all about me for once. I am going to give myself every form of pleasure possible.

Honestly, I think I might be freaking out the sales clerk, for I'm sure there's a bit of a manic glint in my eyes as I pile item upon item onto her counter, a last-minute customer on a mad, perverted shopping spree just minutes before they close up shop for the holidays. I'm sort of grateful that I'm wearing a mask so she can't see what I really look like. This is a pretty over-the-top set of purchases, and I know it.

As she hands me my bags and wishes me "Happy Holidays," it strikes me as illogical that the government is forbidding us from seeing each other socially, but at the same time, we're being encouraged to support local businesses and shop till we drop to support the faltering economy. I can exchange holiday wishes in person with this random saleslady but not my own mother? No wonder we need the "essential services" of sex shops and liquor stores and weed dispensaries to get us through this period of enforced solitude. I mean, I get it, and I obey all the health directives, but it's sort of crazy-making.

Even so, in the midst of this surreal nightmare of a plague-ridden Christmas, I actually find myself humming on the way home. I dump all my discreet black bags under the tree and stir up some mulled wine on the stove. This isn't going to be so bad after all. Fuck Tara. Fuck everyone and everything. I am gonna get rip-roaring drunk and have a zillion orgasms. Not too shabby for a Christmas Eve. And don't I have more chocolate somewhere?

I rummage through my cupboards and find some, as well as other candy, which I put in pretty bowls and set out on end table beside the couch. I should really make dinner, but surely I can live off sugar, alcohol, and masturbation for one night. I plug in the Christmas lights, turn on the gas fireplace, and find a festive playlist to enjoy for the evening. Things look downright cozy. I think about what else I might need and run upstairs for more supplies, ultimately returning with a couple of soft blankets, which I lay on the couch, as well as some candles, which I light on the fireplace mantel. I think about lighting the incense Tara and I bought, but the thought makes me start to tear up, and I quickly squash that idea. I look around and assess. Yes, this is a perfect set-up for a lovely night of loving myself, if sadly no one else.

I look at what I am wearing and am horrified to realize I went to the sex shop in old sweats and no bra. Wow. I am really in a funk. And when was the last time I showered? Shit. I turn off the fireplace and the stove, where the wine has been mulling on low heat. I carry the candles upstairs and place them on the bathroom counter, then peel off my dirty old clothes and turn on the shower. There's really nothing like a hot shower to wash away whatever is bothering me and help me start again, fresh and new. I just stand under the spray and allow the water to flow over my skin, making it feel alive again. I take a moment to appreciate the time and money I invested in laser hair removal because if I hadn't done that two years ago, I'd be spending significant time right now dealing with the ramifications of ignoring my personal hygiene for days. It was a blessed day when I threw away all my razors.

I look at my array of body washes and pick one that will perk me up. It smells of peppermint and lavender, a scent that always gives me a happy kind of energy. I lather it on my body generously, lingering and appreciating my curves. This strong healthy body has gotten me through so much. I scrub my hair, then put on a rich conditioner to soak for a few minutes while I adjust the shower to the hand-held nozzle, using it to bring targeted warmth to different parts of my body. I linger in some parts more than others. Like every woman alive probably does.

Once I feel nice and fresh and clean, before the heat becomes too much, I rinse out my hair and turn off the shower, wrap my hair and my body in some big fluffy towels and pad to the closet to pick an outfit for the night. It's not much of a conundrum. I know before I open the door. I have this emerald green slip that seems appropriately merry, and so I don my gay apparel and slip back into the still-steamy bathroom to appraise my appearance.

I have always thought of myself as an average level of pretty, but my lovers always insist I am too hard on myself. I try to be objective now, scrutinizing myself in the mirror, but as usual, I focus on my shortcomings. For one thing, I'm short. But even as I think it, I can hear lovers past rephrasing it as "petite." "Bite-sized." "A perfect little spoon."

It's funny how the things I don't love in myself can be the very source of appeal for another. Plenty of women have loved me for my small stature. "It makes me feel big and butch," one even joked. So while I might fantasize about being elegantly tall and easily able to reach things high up on a shelf, I have to admit that being smaller has, in fact, drawn a few ladies in.

Then there are my boobs, which I also find too small. Once again, though, I can hear my lovers reminding me that tiny boobs are often part and parcel of being thin, something many women envy about my physique. And small boobs have their own appeal, I have to admit. I can go braless whenever I want to without any discomfort. Plus, they're still perky, even though I'm no longer in my twenties. Right now, the nipples are tight, pushing against the fabric of my slip, a plaid green number that I thought was hilariously femme lesbian when I found it. A little plaid and a little lace. Femme-dyke, all right.

My blond hair hangs in dripping strings about my face, so I run a brush through it and take a moment to appreciate my hair, which I have always loved. I've never once cut it short, despite feeling pressure from the queer community to look a certain way. My hair is my crowning glory, and I'll always keep it long. I like having a mane. I consider it a source of secret, feminine strength, kind of like Samson's. My outfit is decidedly lacking in seasonal accessories, though, so I slap an elf hat on my head and pose seductively in the mirror. Pleased with my imperfectly pretty, sexy elf self, I grab the candles and head back downstairs for an evening of pleasure.

I begin by turning the fireplace and stove back on, give the wine a stir, and then feel a different kind of stir between my thighs when I think of all those presents waiting to be unboxed beneath the Christmas tree. I leave the wine on low and head to the stash to unwrap my first gift to myself. Where to begin? I decide to let fate choose and reach into a bag, feel around, and withdraw a random package. I chose it because it's smaller than the rest, and now I see why.

Nipple clamps, huh? Can't say I've ever tried those. I extricate the little torture devices and look them over. Two little black rubber tips on what look like tweezers on the end of a chain connected to the same thing on the other side. With sliding rings to control the pressure of the pinch on both ends.

I need wine for this and head to the kitchen to fill a cup. The wine is warm and wonderfully spiced as it makes my way down my throat. Luckily, I remember to close my kitchen blinds before I pop out my tits in the kitchen. I laugh to myself as I try to affix the clamps. It's a weird sensation. Not exactly sexy, but novel and interesting nonetheless. I give them an exploratory little tug and feel a dull ache. My nipples have never been particularly sensitive, so I'm not sure what to expect. But it turns me on to be trying something new and to have my tits out and enchained in the kitchen, drinking wine all by myself on Christmas Eve. Rather than sad, it strikes me as kinky and fun, and I swagger to the living room to unwrap another gift. I tighten the sliding rings a bit, then rummage for another new item to try.

It's a vibrator with "thrusting action." I don't know exactly what that means, but I certainly like a good thrusting, so I had thrown it on the counter with the rest of my haul. I remove it from its packaging, and my heart sinks. It needs to charge. Fuck my life. They'll all need to charge, most likely.

What was I thinking? I grab my laptop and plug the toy into the USB port. I dump the rest of the bags, find all the toys that will need a charge, and get them going.

The nipple clamps are starting to irritate me, so I take them off and am surprised at the pleasure from the relief that floods me when they're removed. I rub my breasts to dissipate the strange sensations, unsure whether I like them or not.

My very favorite Christmas carol is playing, a vintage Hawaiian-themed one, so I drink some more wine and dance around, singing to myself, tits jiggling along to the tune as I hula about the room. A lot of women would *love* to find this under their Christmas tree, I think: a half-drunk, half-naked, very horny, slightly woebegone vixen of an elf in festive lingerie. Surely, some sexy woman somewhere has that on her Christmas wish list. So what if Tara brushed me off with a text mere days before the most wonderful time of the year? So what? I'm a strong independent woman, and I don't need her, I think. Her loss.

I remember the candy and grab a handful as I plop down on the couch in decidedly unladylike fashion to stuff my face.

Then I spy a box that hasn't been opened and slink over to it, dusting sugar crumbs off my hands along the way. This one's a glass dildo with a beautiful blue twirling pattern around the shaft. At least there's one toy that won't need to be plugged in. I hold it firmly in my hands and admire its shape. I like the smooth cold texture. I rub it experimentally across my nipples and enjoy the sensation, which inspires a slight shiver of delight. But didn't I read on the package that it can be used for temperature play? I have one vibrator currently charging that has a warming function, so maybe I should alternate between them? I decide to stick the glass dildo in the fridge and save it for later. It will be like fucking an icicle, I think and laugh merrily. I unplug the warming one to see if it's charged enough to use yet, but it fizzles out after barely a few seconds of vibration. And now that I really look at it, it seems disappointingly thin. I like me some girth. I'm a three fingers kind of girl. Surprisingly, perhaps, for my tiny frame, but I can take a lot.

I notice that the control panel on the vibe with thrusting action has stopped lighting up, and I unplug it from the charging port with some hope. When I jab at a random button, it starts to vibrate nicely and doesn't fizzle out. Yes! Finally!

And then my other very, very favorite Christmas carol comes on the playlist. Okay, I have a lot of favorite carols. Did I not already mention that I love Christmas? I squeal and rush to turn up the volume. It's a stupid, silly, preposterous song about wanting a hippopotamus for the holidays, and I march about, belting it out into my new vibe like it's a microphone. No one is around, and if I want to be ridiculous, there's no one to stop me. I spill some wine but ignore it until the song ends since hardwood floors are forgiving. Eventually, the best Christmas song ever does indeed come to an end, so I fulfill my duties as a responsible homeowner and clean up the spill. Then promptly fill up my cup with some more wine and return to the vibe, curious.

I start punching buttons and am surprised when the vibrator begins emitting a loud squeaking sound. What's more alarming, it begins extending then plunging its silicone head up and down and up and down in a lewd robotic imitation of fucking motions. It looks and sounds so comical that I burst out laughing. I can't bring myself to use it. It would be like being fucked by a clown, I think and then shudder at that nightmarish image. Eek! I throw the vibe dramatically into a corner and plop back down on the couch for some chocolate.

So far, I have not had much luck. But then I remember that one of these contraptions was actually recommended to me by the saleslady, and I go to check to see if it's ready. Its charge light has stopped blinking. Now, according to the clerk, this little number has "revolutionized" sex toys. I pick up the instruction manual and read about how it provides direct clitoral stimulation using suction and air pulsation instead of vibration. Well, it's certainly shaped differently than most of the sex toys I've seen. It's a sort of pink oval with a hole that you're supposed to place over your clit, and then supposedly, it will give you a whole new kind of orgasm, which certainly sounds good to me.

I rev it up. It makes an odd sound and creates a slight tugging, suction sensation when I place my finger tentatively on the hole. I take one last swig of wine, then lie back on the couch, prepared to finally try out one of these babies properly.

It seems weird to just slap it on my clit, so I use my hand for a bit first to get in the mood. Touching myself feels good, both relaxing and exciting at the same time. I stare at the colorful lights on the tree and just allow myself to drift off into pleasure. I marvel at the softness of a woman's lips. I enjoy touching my lovers there so much and try to find that same awe and enjoyment while touching my own lips. Finding the right pressure and speed and rhythm to make a woman moan is a thrilling kind of amatory hunt. Oddly, it's a little harder with myself. I've always struggled to fully relax into masturbating. I rarely come from it and hardly ever do it. And yet I'm super orgasmic with a lover. It's just so different and so much more intense when the sensations are wrapped up in my feelings for someone else.

My pussy is primed and ready, though, so I place the toy gently next to my clit. It gives a feeling like a quick little flick of the tongue when someone goes down on you. But not as wet and soft or fluid. Again, the air puffs, short and quick, at my sensitive clit. I'm not sure about it but try to let go and enjoy. It's difficult. It's too focused purely on my clitoris. I like a lover who uses her mouth on my entire vulva, lavishing attention on my mound, lips, clit, vagina, everything. This feels oddly clinical. Too precise. And I don't like the clicking sound it's making.

I get frustrated and throw it away. I forget to turn it off first, though, and the annoying clicking sound continues, taunting me. I growl, scramble out from under my pile of blankets, and scrounge around for the stupid thing. When I finally find and silence it, I promptly burst into tears. Hundreds of dollars spent and nary an orgasm to be found? Is the universe really going to be this awful to me? Is getting dumped just before Christmas not punishment enough for whatever karmic crimes I have committed?

Just then, a blinking light catches my attention, and I swear I hear a magical tinkling sound, like in a cheesy Christmas movie when the main character is being alerted to a miracle about to happen. If I wasn't already inside, I'd expect super fluffy snow to start falling softly about me as the musical score begins to build toward the moment of holiday goodwill and cheer that everyone has been waiting for.

It's the first vibrator that I picked up. The one that originally caught my eye when I was with Tara. Evidently, it's now finished charging too and just waiting for me to assess its efficacy. Will it let me down too? Like everything else about this shitty Christmas Eve? I worry it will. And yet, I have an irrepressible feeling that it might just be "the one." Maybe vibrators are like women, and you have to keep searching until you find the one that's just right for you.

I feel like some kind of pervy Goldilocks as I detach it from my laptop and skeptically press a few buttons. It's a bunny-ears vibe. A classic, according to the packaging. Although it feels sort of strange to be getting off to a forest-animal-inspired sex aid, I'm eager to try it out and settle into my cushy blankets to give it a go.

The combination of being comfortably filled by the dildo while having my clit stimulated by the vibrating ears is a winning one for me. *Wow. Yes.* Evidently, I'm a classic kind of girl. It's definitely doing the trick. I watch the flames of the fireplace for a while, then close my eyes as sexy images start to flood through my brain. That's the thing. I need to think about specific people to get off. The physical stimulation is helpful, but to truly push me over the precipice into orgasm, I need more. A feeling of love. Of being wanted and wanting. This is why masturbation rarely works for me. But maybe I can *remember* those feelings. And maybe it won't hurt so much to remember them now that so many endorphins are flooding my system.

I let my mind float back to my first girlfriend. Samira. University. The Young Feminists Club. Damn, she was so smart and politicized and fiery. She had an opinion about everything. I loved listening to her rant almost as much as I loved going down on her. If I really focus, I can remember the feeling of her hands on me. The jittery excitement in my belly as she concentrated her immensely capable hands on my pleasure. She was a steady burn. A slow build-up in intensity. Unrelenting. Unstoppable. *Yes...*

And then there was Frankie. What a beautiful mistake she was. All wrong for me but such a fox. Sly and mischievous and super sexy. Never one to stay. Never one to apologize for being exactly who she was. I learned a lot from her. Her hands were always firm. Often forceful. Sometimes sneaky. I can feel them on me still too.

One by one, I flit through images of my past lovers. Feel their energy and bodies once more. I tremble on the edge of orgasm. *So close. So close.* But somehow, exasperatingly, not quite close enough.

Then I picture them all. Here with me. Now. In various states of undress. Every single woman I've loved over the past two decades, all here to please me. Right now. In my moment of need. A fantasy, all-girl gang-bang, with me as its star. *Yes!*

My legs start to shake. I'm almost there. A small, judgy part of myself reprimands me for going too far, but I quickly shush it. A fantasy is a fantasy, and I'm entitled to mine, especially tonight, no matter how far gone it is. How wild. Because it is wild, and that's the appeal. Imagining all of them.

Just as loving and hot and desirous as I remember in our best moments. Together. Taking turns loving me. Some competing to outdo each other in a friendly sort of way. But all of them here for me. For *my* pleasure. Wanting me to be happy. Giving to me. Taking care of my needs for once. And somehow, I feel uncharacteristically open to receive all that love without feeling guilty. It's a gift that I can't and don't want to deny. I take it and take it. A greedy little pillow princess being spoiled with attention. Kissing this one's lips, feeling up that one's tits, squeezing that one's bottom. And hands. So many hands on me. Feeling me everywhere. Everywhere. All of them. With me. Inside me. *Yes. Yeeeessss!*

I cry out, unable to hold back as the orgasm rocks my frame. It's longer and more powerful than usual, and I keep expecting it to abate, but it keeps going, and I start laughing because I'm all mixed up: happy and sad and confused and surprised. But then finally it starts to die down, and I can catch my breath, reorient myself to reality. I turn off the vibe and snuggle beneath the covers to ride out the aftershocks of one of the most satisfying orgasms of my life. My heartbeat slows, and I find myself feeling sleepy. I think about getting up to turn everything off, but I really can't be bothered. Let it be, I think. Just let it all be.

Tara pops into my head. A brief, unpleasant sensation that pokes at but cannot destroy my precious little bubble of happiness. I expected to have a long-term partner by now, and the thought that I don't should pain me. But somehow, in this moment, it doesn't. My body is deeply sated. I feel awash in good feelings. This isn't the Christmas I wanted, but I'm okay. I can take care of myself as much as other people. *I'm okay.*

I start to drift off to sleep, secure in the memory of how all these strong and beautiful women have loved me. I'm still looking for my right fit. For the one. But I keep faith. I believe. I trust I'll find her eventually, and when I do, I will shower her with affection and presents and spoil her to the core with caretaking because that's how I know to love.

But until then, I'll do the same for myself. Because I deserve that too.

The last thing I hear is the soft sound of my very, very, very favorite Christmas carol lulling me to a peaceful rest.

PART FOUR: WRESTLING WITH DESIRE
STRUGGLE EROTICA

BOSSY

I am a smart, capable, accomplished woman. I tend to get what I want. At least nowadays. But getting here wasn't easy. Because I used to be a smart, capable little girl, and like most little girls, I had to learn how to get shit done without earning the dreaded label of being "too bossy." "Bossy" confused the younger me until I figured out, on some subconscious level, that it was something girls got called when they were too strong, too clever, too skillful. So I learned to hide those things about myself. To be just the right, non-threatening amount of talented and to direct attention for any of my success to other people's influence. For the longest time, I didn't even realize I was doing this.

A turning point came in my late thirties. Hanging out with friends of ours, another couple, drinking and ostensibly playing euchre, I stumbled into a rediscovery of the heady justness of being a woman who spoke her mind with zero fucks. Which was ironic because it was an abundant literal giving of passionate fucks that led to this revival.

I had been complaining about my latest haircut, explaining to my friends why I didn't tell my hairdresser that I was unhappy with it. That was when Kendra exploded. "You're paying a *professional*. Don't leave until you get what you want." Kendra was the femme half of our best friend couple. She was loud, larger than life, and unapologetic about being a big woman with strong opinions about, well…everything. Her boldness both scared me and drew me to her. Ash, her partner, was more even-keeled. Patient. The stereotypical strong but silent butch type. So they fit well together. A study in contrasts.

"She even tipped her," Jade chimed in mischievously, which earned her an irritated glare from me.

"Jen, seriously," Kendra started, gesturing wildly with her empty wineglass. "You've got to learn to speak up. You can't go your whole life being afraid to express an opinion or ask for what you want. Like right now, I want a refill. You don't see me hesitating to say, 'Babe, top me up.'"

"I'm not afraid," I protested as Ash promptly rose to fill her glass with a good-natured grin. She grabbed mine on the way to the kitchen too.

"Oh, please, Jennifer. I've been your friend for like, what, eight years now? I've heard you tell the same story a million times. You just need to practice…wait. Actually, that's it."

She was tipsy, and her eyes lit up, so I knew that whatever idea just popped into her head, it was going to direct our evening, as her whims usually did, often with amusing results.

Ash returned from the kitchen, handed the glasses over, then settled back into her chair. Kendra stared fixedly at her until she said, "What?"

"I think our friend Jen needs an intervention. A lesson in asking for what she wants. How about you bois treat us girls to a little massage?"

We all looked at each other. "Sure," Jade answered, getting up to move closer to me, but as she passed, Kendra grabbed her arm.

"No. You do me. Ash will do her. If everyone's okay with that?"

Heat flushed through me, and I could see by Jade's face that she was having the same reaction. We had always found Kendra and Ash super attractive. They were bigger women who wore their curves well, taking up space confidently in a way that defied expectations. I always admired the way their fullness of flesh positively dared everyone not to find them sumptuous. As skinnier women who constantly worried about their weight, Jade and I both found that refreshing. And alluring. We weren't the kind of couple who hid things like that from each other. We shared openly when we thought someone was hot. And we had joked around in the past about how dangerous it would be to drink too much with them. I knew from Jade's face that she was remembering the same conversation. Her eyes sought mine, and I nodded and so did she and so did Ash. And so…that was that. Ash made her way over and settled beside me on the couch.

Then Kendra started talking to Ash in French, an annoying habit they had of making jokes and sharing secrets in a language we didn't know. Or at least didn't remember. I mean, everyone learned French in school in Canada, but most Anglophones tended to forget it all upon graduation. Not Ash and Kendra. Usually, Jade would just join in, pretending to follow along and making up ridiculously pompous-sounding nonsense— bonjour croissant ballet moustache—but this situation was too delicate. So we just awkwardly sat there, waiting.

Then Ash's hands were on my shoulders, kneading very gently. I knew she had strong hands. I'd stared at them often enough. But she was barely touching me. Did she not want to be doing this? Did she think I was too tiny or—

"How's it going over there?" Kendra asked. "Are you enjoying Ash's touch, Jen?"

I mumbled a yes, not wanting the attention.

"Really? And how's the pressure? Too hard for you?" I noticed her eyes were twinkling playfully. Did she tell Ash to give me a piss-poor massage? Was that what she was up to? Making me ask for more pressure? Fine, I could do that.

"I could handle more pressure, um, actually," I said awkwardly, afraid of hurting Ash's feelings. Kendra barked something in French, and Ash practically snapped my neck with the pressure. I gasped and without hesitating blurted, "A little softer."

Ash chuckled and whispered "Good job" in my ear before massaging me with just the right amount of strong and knowing pressure. Before long, I lost myself in the sensations, in the deliciousness of letting go, in the novelty of new touch, then was startled to look up and see Kendra studying me intently.

"Your girlfriend has good hands," she drawled.

"Yes, she does," I admitted, smiling at Jade.

"Mine too, though, wouldn't you say?"

"Definitely."

There was undeniable erotic tension connecting all of us now. I was sure everyone could feel it. The bois kept kneading our flesh in silence, waiting, and I felt incredibly anxious and excited, uncertain as to where Kendra intended to take this.

"That was a good start. But if you're going to be assertive like me, you need more experience bossing people around. Ash likes to be bossed around by a pretty woman, don't you, Ash?"

Ash didn't answer, but she made a sound in the back of her throat, and I assumed she was smiling.

"Okay, Jen, I'm the boss, and you're my assistant. I'm teaching you to lead. And we're going to tell these handsome butches exactly how to please us. They're here to serve our every need. Sound good?"

"Sounds like every day," Ash muttered, and we all laughed.

"Now, what shall we have them do?" Kendra said.

But it was too much pressure. Too terrifyingly exciting. I couldn't even make eye contact. So I just looked down and waited.

"I want to watch them wrestle," Kendra said. "Who do you think would win?"

Jade and Ash both stopped massaging and started laughing and sizing each other up rather dramatically. I laughed along.

"Seriously, should we have them wrestle? Would you like to see that, Jen?"

"Yeah, definitely." Then I added without thinking: "But they should be topless."

This got a huge reaction, and Jade bounded over to kiss me and playfully raise my glass to my lips, saying, "That's it. Keep drinking, baby."

Ash and Jade knew exactly how to play this up. They were super charming, hamming it up, being mildly silly but with fiercely sexy undertones. They liked being on display for a highly appreciative crowd of two. They postured and flexed. Jade removed Ash's belt, making a big production of it and snapping it loudly once it was off.

"I think our lovely ladies should do the rest," Jade offered. Ash nodded and waited to see where Jade would head. Jade looked at me, then made her way to Kendra. She checked in with her eyes. I smiled. Ash followed suit and kneeled before me on the couch.

"Would you like to unbutton me?"

I couldn't breathe. The world shrank down to my hesitant fingers on her shirt, revealing her secret self button by button by button by button. Until she was undone, exposed, and my heart was beating wildly. I risked looking at her face and saw that she wanted to kiss me as much as I did her. My eyes lingered on her mouth, so tantalizingly close, her lips, so soft and inviting.

Ever conscious of our partners, my eyes strayed across the room to Jade, who had flung off her T-shirt with enthusiasm and was smirking and raising her arms above her head, offering Kendra the task of removing her black sports bra. Kendra was not one to hesitate. Her manicured fingers traced Jade's midriff then worked their way under her bra, freeing her tight, pert breasts from their restraint. She flung the bra away with eager abandon.

Their eye contact smoldered. Jade looked wicked hot

kneeling before another pretty femme. I've always loved the contrast she embodies, how her edgy short hair and androgynous clothing mask her wholly female body, like a secret awaiting unwrapping. At times, the way she holds herself can suggest boyish cockiness, and yet the way she comports herself always expresses a gentle, feminine core. The interplay in her gender expression, the contradiction, was what tended to get me. This night was no different. She kneeled teasingly before Kendra, her dark eyes twinkling roguishly, hands firmly on her hips, her body opened with self-assured poise to Kendra's keen, appraising gaze. I felt myself start to get wet just watching them.

Then Kendra began directing the show. Ash broke obediently away to play her part, and I was left bereft. Until she and Jade started grappling on the living room floor in a memorably funny and exhilarating way. It was playful but edged with real eroticism as they tussled about before us to my silent delight and Kendra's very vocal appreciation, instructions, and taunting. Their bodies came together in queer and inspiring configurations of straining muscle and bouncing curve. A new study in contrasts with Jade's taut, athletic frame in ever-shifting juxtaposition with Ash's more voluptuous physique. Kendra hooted enthusiastically, and I stared elatedly as they struggled for dominance. Ash was significantly bigger than Jade, so it was no surprise when she won, panting and sweaty, both of them smiling and proud.

But Kendra was a few glasses in, and more inspiration had clearly struck. She blurted out unabashedly, "That was a good show, but I want to see you two make out."

My heart skipped a beat. Or five.

"What are we now, your porn stars?" Ash asked, smiling wryly.

"Yes, you're my porn stars. Exactly. I'm the director, and you two have to make out however I say."

Jade piped up. "I thought this was about Jen learning to give orders. Why isn't she the director?"

"Because Jen is the fluffer, that's why."

"Lesbians don't need fluffers," Jade exclaimed.

Kendra gave Jade her most condescending look as she explained, "Lesbians don't *need* fluffers, but that doesn't mean they don't *want* fluffers."

I watched Jade anxiously, curious about her reaction. All her partners had been feminine, so I wasn't sure how she would feel about making out with another butch. And indeed, I saw in her face that she was struggling with mixed emotions.

"I'd like to establish ground rules," she finally said. "Can we keep things above the belt? At least for now." Ash nodded, and Kendra clapped her hands with determination.

"Okay, okay. Now what should we have you two do?" She was in her element. Giving orders, bustling about rearranging the set, and grabbing extremely random props. She was shouting orders to a nonexistent crew, using film terms that probably no one understood, but it kept everyone laughing. When we weren't holding our breath. Because when Ash and Jade finally kissed, it was *toe-tinglingly hot*.

I'd never seen my partner make out with someone else, and it was like falling for her all over again, watching the way she moved her toned, tanned body with such easy confidence. I didn't feel jealous at all. I felt riveted. I felt lucky to call her mine. I felt reinspired to love every little bit of her. No matter how much I loved a partner, over time, it was easy to forget to really look at them. Incomparable intimacy came with a quality long-term partnership, but the price of that close connection was the mystery and distance that fueled certain kinds of desire. Watching my partner make out with someone else helped me see her anew. It gave me the distance to recognize once again just how much I did and did not know her. Her touch with Ash was both different and familiar all at once. It was deliciously uncanny in a way that felt unsettling and stirring. Ash aroused new things in Jade and in me, as a result.

I'd also never really seen two masculine women together. It was thrilling to witness something so rare and powerful. It was everything I liked in a dyke but...*doubled*...and I was wondering if this multiplication of the object of desire was why straight guys liked girl-on-girl porn, when Kendra rudely interrupted my rapture at the vision with a harsh, "Cut. Cut. I said cut, goddammit!" She used a hardcover book like a clapperboard to interrupt them. "This isn't working," she said. "Ash needs fluffing."

I realized with a start that she was calling me into the scene, and I froze in terror. I just wanted to watch and revel from the safety of the sidelines, but the spotlight was clearly on me now.

"Me too. I need fluffing too." Jade smirked, sidling up to me. "Come on, baby. Fluff me." She laughed invitingly, but I couldn't. I didn't know what the hell a lesbian fluffer would even do. I started to sweat and freak out, but then Ash was behind me, and Jade was before me, and *I* didn't have to decide anything because *they* decided that I needed to be in the middle of a decidedly succulent butch sandwich.

They smelled delicious, and their hands, so many hands, were so many places, feeling me every which way and where. I couldn't focus. I didn't fight it. I just melted into the sensation of something so amazing that it had never even crossed my mind before that moment as a real possibility within the livable realm of sensual pleasure. Something so achingly beautiful and unique that I could intimately know. Something unthinkably, staggeringly marvelous. *That* was a butch sandwich. Warm breath on my neck. Teeth on my earlobe. Hands cupping my breasts, rubbing my thighs. *Whose? Wow. Oh my God.*

At some point, I became aware of Kendra crossing her arms and scrutinizing the scene. I struggled to focus on what she was saying. "This isn't in the script, but it's fine. It's fine. We'll fix it in post. A good director knows when to let her actors improvise." She moved to her chair and sipped her wine, watching us and unbuttoning her blouse. "Upstart little fluffer," she muttered as she reached into her shirt, presumably to play with her nipples as she watched us. I heard Ash invite her in, but she demurred. "Nope. This is all Jen. Make her tell you what she wants."

"What do you want?" Ash whispered into my ear, her fingers waiting on the clasp at the front of my push-up bra.

I looked Jade in the eyes and saw open enthusiasm. "I want you both to fuck me," I admitted as Ash released the clasp and my tits burst free, seeming to free the last of our restraint along with them.

"That's my girl," Jade said with a growl as she removed my pants and panties with Ash's eager assistance.

It wasn't just how our bodies came together, who did what to whom and how. I opened more than my legs; I opened my mind. Not only to new sensations but also to new possibilities of being. I mean what literally happened was that two women I respected took turns worshipping my body. Worked together to see just how much pleasure I could take. Occasionally tried to outdo each other in a friendly, mildly competitive way.

But I learned things too. A silly but surprising example: I always thought that scissoring was made-up bullshit invented by straight men. None of my lovers had ever placed their pussies on mine. Generally grinding, yes. Specifically scissoring like the chicks in girl-on-girl porn, no. So when Ash put one of my legs up on her shoulder and began moving herself, slick and rhythmic, against me, I was taken aback. Usually, if my legs were dangling over some dyke's shoulders, there was a strap-on involved. I thought I might miss the sensation of penetration, but this was so novel, this warm, wet softness shared between us, that I felt no lack. Matching my breath and movement to the level of intensity she was emitting, my legs started to shake, sweat broke out on my skin, and I started to feel bold.

"I want to see you two kiss," I commanded.

They smiled and went for it with gusto. I watched them lock lips over me, one of Jade's strong hands grabbing the back of Ash's head, the other still squeezing my breast. Their kissing was fierce. Wild. A continuation of the wrestling in some strange way, as they met each other's power with equal power. Fuck! Why did we never see images like this? I wondered briefly, somewhere in the back of my mind, as I felt my wetness flood. This was exceptional. And I was blessed to be witness to it. This strange carnality of boi-on-boi competition.

Luckily, I was brought out of my head by Ash's physical insistence. I felt her pelvis push hard against me and not relent. It pulsated and began to spasm. A low growl escaped her lips, and it was so very fine and feral that my body responded in kind, her sensuality and freedom inspiring my own speedy release as our bodies came together in perfect, rare harmony. An unexpected gift.

Then she crashed down beside me, struggling to catch her breath and craning her neck to check in with Kendra. Who was clearly in the midst of her own rather flamboyant crescendo. I wasn't sure her chair was going to survive the tumult.

I looked to Jade, who had snuggled down onto the other side of me, smiling slyly as she traced her hand along my face and kissed me sweetly. "You're so sexy," she whispered.

"I agree," Ash replied.

"You're both amazing," I responded, truly in awe.

"Yeah. Okay. I admit it. Those were some pretty impressive moves," Jade conceded playfully.

"It's all in the hips," Ash replied, winking.

"Yes, yes, everyone's incredible," Kendra said, getting up noisily and throwing a blanket our way. "Who needs a refill?"

She shuffled off to the kitchen to replenish our drinks while the three of us snuggled under the blanket, giggling and giddy like schoolgirls. Drunk on more than the alcohol.

How could we not be giddy? There were tits everywhere. So many tits. All over me. *My own. Hers. Hers. My own? Hers. More. And hands. Oh my God.*

By the time Kendra came back, we were already well into round two, which earned us a huffy "Wait till I shout 'action,' at least. Show some respect for film set protocol." We invited her in, but she was still into her game and wanted only to watch.

"Watching is kind of her thing," Ash explained, helping me feel more comfortable with her voyeuristic distance.

"What do you want, Jen?" Jade cooed in my ear.

I didn't hesitate. "I still want you both to fuck me. But at the same time."

And so they did. Taking turns placing their hands on my pussy. Working in tandem. Stroking my clit. Massaging my vulva. Slapping. Penetrating. Thoroughly enjoying. Jokingly pushing each other's hands out of the way. Getting cocky.

"Watch this."

"Naw, you gotta use three fingers."

"It's all about the twist."

"You said it was all about the hips."

"Can't be a one-trick pony."

Eventually, Jade straddled my face, burying all my senses in her pussy. The sweet familiar scent, taste, and feel of her engulfed me as the sound of her moans filled my ears. Meanwhile, Ash's strong and nimble fingers filled my cunt with new sensations. Her mouth teased my clit. I found myself mimicking her rhythms and moves so that everything her tongue played out on my clit moved its way through my flesh to Jade's. Quick, powerful, nonstop flicks of the tongue. Slow, sumptuous swirls encircling the inner lips. Vigorous, head-shaking direct pressure. Coy, warm breath playfully teasing my pussy. Whatever I was given, I passed on, feeling it both in myself and in my partner. It wasn't something I did consciously but a pattern that I fell into, one that felt wonderfully right. In time, Ash added in suction, drawing my clit into her mouth and holding it there, steady and strong, as her fingers thrust forcefully within me, pushing me to the edge of climax and holding me there in the most agonizingly blissful way.

"At the same time," I repeated. And they finally caught on, switching gears smoothly to meet me where I was at. They both came inside me and synchronized their rhythms. I didn't last more than three minutes, thinking of them both with their fingers inside me together, feeling them meet in my most intimate place. Fulfilling the deepest of my secrets, a desire so very innermost.

I let out a long luxurious sigh. Stretched like a cat. "Oh my God, I don't think I could possibly handle any more. Who's next?"

"Done already, princess?" Jade teased.

"You can't be done yet," Ash said. "I haven't even had a chance to show off my signature move."

I started to protest, uncomfortable about being the center of attention for so long. I'd never shake a reputation for being a pillow princess if I kept this up. But on and on it went. Banter. Pleasure. Playfulness. Orgasm. And learning.

At one point, I turned to Ash. "Can I go down on you?" No beating around the proverbial bush. No needing to be prodded to ask for what I wanted. Just a confident, direct request. So I was pleasing her with my mouth when Kendra finally decided to step in.

"You've got to pinch her nipples really hard if you want her to come." She put down her glass and walked over. Kneeled. Looked hungrily at me and commanded, "Kiss me. I want to taste my girlfriend on your lips."

Hotter words were never spoken. And because I was such

a fast learner, I didn't hesitate to agree, adding, "Okay, but only if you return the favor with my girlfriend."

Like I said, I was a smart, capable, accomplished woman. A bossy femme learning to reclaim her strong will. And I tended to get what I wanted.

MISS BLACK AND MS. HUNT

Author's Note: One of the first times that the word "gay" was used as a code word for same-sex love was in 1922 in a short story called "Miss Furre and Miss Skeene," written by Gertrude Stein. She was playing around with perspective at the time, showing one subject from multiple viewpoints in literature, just as Pablo Picasso was doing with painting. This piece takes inspiration from Stein's pioneering, experimental queer story.

Ms. Hunt

Gym teachers. I've always had a thing for gym teachers. It's the self-assurance in their own bodies that gets me. And the whistle. The yelling of instructions. Do this. Do that. Not like that, like this. Every queer schoolgirl has had a crush on her gym teacher. Except now I'm a teacher, and she's my colleague, and we're not supposed to call it gym anymore. That's a faux pas. It's Physical *Education*. Stress on the education, on this being a legitimate subject. But all I know is that I dream of being subject to her "physical education." Telling my body what to do. How to win. *Score!*

It's the last week of class before summer break. No one's really teaching anymore. So I bring the girls outside to sit under a tree and socialize under the pretense of reading. We did silent reading outdoors often enough that no one will question it. They're all abuzz with summer plans and gossip and boys, and I can sit quietly and watch her, Miss Black, leading a loose game of soccer for one of her last classes. She holds up a hand and smiles to signal that she sees me. I return the gesture, settle down, and pretend to read while sneaking glimpses of her toned, tanned body and drifting off into fantasies.

I was never good at sports. I was curvy and self-conscious around athletic girls, those jock girls who seemed to get each other in a way that excludes me. Their ease in their own skin, their instinctive know-how, their moves and competence, the aggression that lay in wait under a surface smoothed with jokes and camaraderie. I wanted to be part of that, but I wasn't like them, and I didn't think they liked me, not in that way. I always feared that when they looked at me, all they saw was that I was fat. That I must have been lazy. Lacking self-discipline.

But I know self-discipline. I've spent my entire life trying to discipline my body and then disciplined my life to make up for failing at it. Trying to be perfect. Smart. Accomplished. Tidy. Nice. And I am. I'm now that nice, pretty, smart girl who is just a little too chubby to be a threat, so all the other girls can still like her. I'm nice and bland. Except that I'm not. In my head at least, my fantasies are rowdy and fierce, outrageously big, like my tits, which I struggle to contain. Yeah, like my tits, my fantasies are so big and outrageous that even I don't know what to do with them. They overwhelm me. Until there's no choice but to surrender to them. Ride them out and just revel in their power until they're exhausted.

And I've got a secret obsession, which is decidedly not a nice girl's obsession. It started when I was bored and horny one night and typed "dyke kink" into Google on a whim. What I found reoriented my entire erotic imagination, has dominated it for a solid month now as I played out different variations on the same theme in my daily dirty daydreams. It's called Ultimate Surrender, an unscripted dyke wrestling match with an...um...unusual scoring scheme and a rather inspiring prize for winning. Three rounds. Points for stripping your opponent and performing certain specific, permitted sexual acts. Forced surrenders. Then in the fourth and final round, winner takes all, all she wants of the loser. With a big strap-on dildo that matches the winner's team colors.

So far in my imaginary wrestling career, I've got a pretty decent win-loss ratio. Primal Kitten and Missy Amazon both kicked my ass. Literally, in the fourth round, my ass was theirs. But I annihilated Tits McGee, whose wrestling skills were nowhere near as impressive as her knockers, which gave even mine a run for their money. The fantasies are outlandish and definitely over-the-top, but fun. They amuse me. I'm watching Miss Black move across the field, and suddenly she's in the mix, the first time I've imagined someone known to me. We're on the mat wearing team bikinis, purple and green, with matching arm and leg bands. The cheesy theme music is playing, and the camera is panning around as we stretch, lingering to get some choice T&A shots as we strain and prepare. The ref, a porn star in a black and white striped bikini top, with short shorts and cute knee socks, interviews us pregame.

I know the shtick. Name. Stats. Strategy. What you'll do to her if you win.

I strike a tough pose for the camera. "Hi. My name's Sassy Peaches. I'm five-four, none-of-your-fucking-business pounds, and my strategy today is to suffocate her with my tits. Maybe get in a little finger blasting. Then in round four, when I win, I'm going to do a bunch of dirty, dirty things to her before we ride off into the sunset together."

Her turn. She strikes an intimidating pose. "Hi. I'm the Ice Vixen. I'm five-six, one hundred and thirty-five pounds, and my strategy is to use genuine wrestling moves because I actually know what the hell I'm doing, unlike all these other pretty girl posers. Grab some popcorn, viewers, 'cuz I'm about to put on a show. She'll be the first to come on the mat. Guaranteed. Then in round four, *when* I win, I'm going to drag her all around the court by her hair and show her just what a winner can do."

It's my fantasy, though, so of course I win the first round. She underestimated my determination and aggression. The element of surprise wins me a number of points before she even fully realizes what's happening.

The ref gives the play-by-play: "Control by purple. Bikini top off. We've got breast fondling…ooh, control lost."

Ice Vixen snaps out of her surprise, and we grapple for control. I've got weight on her, but she's strong. I've got four prior matches under my belt, though, so I pin her quickly again.

"Control by purple again with a reverse schoolgirl pin. Some nice ass smothering going on. Points for bikini bottom lost and…do we? Do we? Yes, yes, we've got pussy rubbing."

Vixen is bucking and wriggling and trying to clamp her legs together, but I've got a good position, and I'm not going anywhere. She's panting and grunting, and I'm not sure if it's from trying to escape the hold or from my fingers on her clit, when the ref chimes in, "Control maintained. We've reached the one-minute mark. Submission is now possible."

I wiggle my ass theatrically in her face as my fingers keep working and ask, "You ready to submit yet?" But when I glance back at her face, I can see that she's no longer really trying to escape, and the bucking is timed to my fingers. I smile and interrupt the rhythm. "You've got to submit this round if you want to finish."

"Fuck you," she growls.

"Mmm…maybe later. For now, just say you submit, and I'll finish this." I push my bikini bottom back on her face and start slapping her pussy playfully. "Ready yet? How 'bout now," I say as I push my fingers inside her. Eventually, she resentfully submits and comes all over the mat. So round one goes to purple.

The second round, she's pissed. No longer holding back. The moment the ref blows the whistle, she's on me, and I can't shake her no matter how I move. We're both sweating, muscles straining, bodies contorting uncomfortably, but we grit our teeth and fight to be on top.

The ref sashays around us, calling out her usual rundown of plays. "Full body control by green with leg scissors. Bikini top off. Our viewers thank you for that, Ice Vixen. And green's going for the bottoms. But purple's fighting it. She's fighting and succeeds. Control lost."

It goes on and on. Control lost. Control maintained. Green. Purple. Face sitting. Forced pussy eating. On and on.

But I want her to win. I want her to fuck me, but I want to struggle first. I want us both to earn it. And we do.

The match goes to green. We're both naked and dishevelled and panting, but the ref makes us stand side by side with her. She raises the Ice Vixen's hand in the air, blowing her whistle and declaring her the winner, while another porn star in fantasy ref gear affixes the winner's strap-on, inserting the bright green dildo into the harness with over-the-top Vanna White–style fanfare.

Now the winner usually humiliates the loser. Makes her suck her big fat cock like the big fat loser that she is. But Ice Vixen isn't so cruel. Just focused. Commanding. She grabs me by the hair for a victory lap of the mat and throws me down in the middle.

"On your knees. Face down. Ass up." She fucks me from behind, grabbing my hair, throwing in a few stinging ass slaps from time to time. She's got stamina. And force. And I've lost all pretence of control, moaning "*Yes*" in time with her thrusts.

"You're better at getting fucked than you are at wrestling," she says. But I can barely hear her. I'm close. I'm on the edge.

"Can I come, please?" I ask, teetering on the brink of orgasm.

"No." She stops thrusting, and I make a sound of desperation. "You haven't earned it yet. Get over here and ride my cock. I want to see your titties bounce."

I obey and clamber over to her, placing her gingerly inside myself, then closing my eyes and finding a rhythm of motion that feels right. She's not thrusting, though. I open my eyes and see she has her arms crossed casually behind her head with a smirk on her face, like she's intent on just sitting back and enjoying the view.

"Get to work," she says, and I do, moving my hips and intentionally bouncing in ways that make my breasts go crazy. If she wants a show, I know how to give one. I'm exhausted, though. My legs are shaking from the strain of the match, and there's a sheen of sweat coating my skin. She barks, "You can do better than that," and I try, but this position isn't really working for me, and tit jiggling looks more fun than it feels. But then it's like she reads my mind and shifts gears.

She grabs my hips, pushing down on them as she thrusts with her hips with crazy ferocity. I grab my tits and hold on, feeling the crescendo of orgasm approaching again. I can feel her eyes staring at me even though I've closed mine. There's a strange sound, and it takes me a while to realize it's me, moaning a moan that's more like a drawn-out wail.

"You can come now," she says...but I'm startled out of the fantasy by movement and remember where I am. The bell must have rung because students are pouring into and out of the school. My own students are gathering their things. I shake myself out of the reverie just in time to notice Miss Black coming toward me. With intention. I panic a bit, realizing I really need to get a hold of myself. I can't go fantasizing about coworkers like that. Not when I'm working. Oh my God she's really coming over here. Control yourself. Control yourself. Control yourself.

❖

Miss Black

She's reading outside with the kids again. I can never focus when she does that. Not that it matters today. Second to last class of the year for this group of girls. They wanted to play soccer, and at this point in the year, as long as they're active, I'm happy. But distracted. She unbalances me. Puts me off my game. She's so sexy in this way that she doesn't realize, which makes it even sexier. She's got that Marilyn Monroe 1950s kinda body, curvy, wholly female. Her breasts are always practically bursting out of her blouses, and I know women well enough to know that must drive her insane, but I fucking love it. It distracts me. I sit in staff meetings with her, trying not to stare at her chest, willing, just willing the buttons to burst with everything in me. And for her part, it's like everything she does is about downplaying and containing that ripe female sensuality that is literally bursting from her seams, from her fleshy hips to her luscious ass to the swell of her chest. That's why it's sexy, man. It's barely restrained.

Monday, she had her hair in a bun and wore these stockings with a seam running up the back, plus these strappy little heels, and I was absolutely beside myself. It was like every naughty librarian fantasy girl I'd ever dreamed about was just click, click, clicking her way down the hall in front of me, her round bottom mesmerizingly inviting in her little black skirt. I had to leave at lunch to go home and jerk off, I was so crazy out-of-control horny. She gets me like that.

I suspect she's the kind of woman who always matches her panties to her bra too. That drives me wild. All that girlie stuff, imagining her lingerie and what she might be wearing underneath her clothes. She probably coordinates her curtains with her throw cushions too. She's that kind of woman. Orderly. Well put together. Sophisticated. If she saw my place, she'd think I was a slob. Maybe I am a slob. A pervy slob who has wicked awesome fantasies about her. About her riding my face like I'm a fucking stallion. About her tying me up and punishing me every time I can't spell a word right. "No, Mississippi has two p's." *Smack!* About fucking her on her desk after school, ungraded papers flying everywhere as I ram into her with my strap-on, her legs over my shoulders with those strappy little heels on. Yeah.

And maybe my boss secretly catches us. Oh yeah. Well, of course the poor fucker would be deeply shocked to see two of his esteemed female staff at this prestigious private school getting it on, but more importantly, he would also be so turned on and impressed and unmanned by my mad strap-on skills that his dick would just shrivel up and fall off. Maybe spontaneously combust. Ashes to ashes. Take that, Principal Fuckwad. And the moral of the story is that he quits, shamed by a couple of muffin munchers, and I finally get an administrator who actually funds my goddamned teams properly. Preferably a female. Who also wears strappy heels. And likes big desks… mmm…I'll think more on that later.

Except, when am I not thinking about Alice Hunt? Look, I think it's stupid when people say that they "just knew" when they met their partners. Love at first sight is a crock. But I definitely felt lust at first sight when I met her at the start of the year. I could immediately imagine fucking her a million different ways, a million different times. I could see us together. Fitting. Sexually. Which is crazy because she's way too smart and classy for some dope like me. But then I think, I might be a dumb jock, but I know how to fuck a lady. And she's exactly that. I can see myself taking her shoe shopping and holding her ridiculously big, color-coordinated purse and picking out paint swatches for our place and enduring all that stupid shit I don't care about just so I can taste her later.

I can imagine birthday sex. Candlelit mutual massage marathons. Weekend long fuck bonanzas. I'd take her in the shower, on the kitchen table, on the hood of my car. Everywhere. We'd have long-term couple sex too...but the good kind. The kind where you are known and seen and loved for exactly who you are. And things might get predictable. But then we'd change it up. Get all dressed up for a party and right before we leave, I'd smack her left ass cheek until it was red and imprinted with my hand. Order her not to wear panties. See if she can stand the asymmetry. The breeze. The anticipation of knowing all night long that her pussy is just waiting for my fingers to find it in some dark corner or unsuspected moment in a breaking point of desire. Yeah.

Sad sex too. Like, shit happens, life sucks, hard times sex, when you turn over to the person you love, tears on your face, and they know to get naked and hold your hand and kiss you everywhere, until you're both crying, but it feels good somehow too. The whole gamut. I can see it all. Because we'd be in it together. And I can imagine that, and maybe that's crazy. Maybe I'm being dense, because a woman like her would never see anything in me, but I've got to try. A year now I've been watching her, the only other out lesbian at the school, and we almost avoid each other, there's so much tension. But tension could be a good sign. So fucking whatever, smack my ass with a metre stick and slap a dunce cap on me, but I think we could work. I could work hard for a woman like that. I spent ten years of my life devoted to excelling at hockey. I could devote another ten to excelling at pleasing her. I know I could. So...fuck it...here goes nothing.

The Gym Teacher and the English Teacher

"Is this seat taken?" Gesturing to the ground beside Ms. Hunt under the tree.

"Yes."

"Yes?"

"No, I mean! No. Sorry." Gathering her things, flustered.

"Reading outside with the kids again?"

"Yes." Ms. Hunt blushes.

"Hmm…funny because the last time I checked, reading required flipping pages. I couldn't help but notice that you've been stuck on the same page the whole time."

"Oh, well I…I guess I was…distracted." More blushing.

"I guess it wasn't a very good book."

"Or the distraction was very good." A pregnant pause.

"Listen, my uh, my friends are bugging me to go to this poetry slam thing with them next weekend. I'm trying to get out of it because I know I probably won't understand what the hell they're talking about, but uh…I was thinking, that's probably your kind of thing, and if you're not busy, and if you're interested…in the slam, I mean…interested in the slam, maybe you could join us and you know, translate the poems into dumb jock–speak." A moment of charged silence. Then a brilliant smile breaks out on Ms. Hunt's face.

"I'll tell you what. Let's make a deal. We'll go with your friends to the slam, and I'll do my best to explain the poems, but only if you take me to a sporting event of your choice. *Without* your friends. And you can explain the game to me. We could…you know…teach each other…"

CAPTIVATED

I had always been a sucker for a pretty woman. My whole life, I found myself in ludicrous situations caused by some cute girl. So it was really not all that surprising when I found myself signing a liability waiver to enter a sensory deprivation tank in a hippie dippie frou-frou spa, because—all too predictably—a pretty woman swore it would do me good. And not just any pretty woman. My far too irresistibly sexy ex-girlfriend, Priyanka Patel. Pri. She of the mauve lips and flighty ways. The one I couldn't stand and couldn't stay away from. Couldn't have and couldn't let go.

She was talking. Saying something about the benefits of antigravity and homeostasis, whatever the hell that was. Spouting flowery nonsense as usual. But damn, that nonsense spouted from tantalizingly gorgeous lips. My eyes lingered over her shapes again, noting them as if for the first time. She was slim, tall, elegantly proportioned, and had an endearing habit of using her hands in melodramatic and graceful gestures whenever she got excited. She got excited a lot.

She had smooth brown skin and dark eyes that twinkled easily with pleasure and mischief. Her hair was shorn to a medium length, much to her conservative Indian parents' chagrin. When they wailed that she would never find a husband with such hair, she promptly dyed the ends dark green in a fashion I later learned was called "ombre," which I could only assume was French for "Fuck you, parental units."

She was still talking. She did that a lot too. Today it was something about the "seven theories of floating," and evidently that had some kind of relationship to "biofeedback" and "neurochemicals," but only the odd word of her speech made it through the obfuscating fog of my desire. I was trying to figure out if today was a bra day or not. Pri occasionally went without, and her tits were so tiny that no one could tell unless they knew to look. I knew to look. I was, in fact, looking hard. But then she turned abruptly and walked away, still nattering on. I rushed to keep up, shifting my gaze to the ripe roundness of her ass cheeks moving most melodically before me.

She opened a door and gestured me inside. *Well, if a pretty woman beckons, I follow.* And thus, I found myself in a compact room with a giant white egg-like tank in the center. My heartbeat sped up. *How the hell do I forget that I am freaking claustrophobic?* Clearly, I didn't really think this through.

"Jess, this is going to be so helpful for you. Tons of athletes use float tanks to relieve joint pain. Zero gravity is *so* good for your mind and body."

I mumbled something incoherent and scanned the room anxiously. There was nothing much else in here but a bench for undressing and a small shower stall in the corner. A basket with pool noodles, ear plugs, and towels. That was it.

"So like I explained earlier, this tank contains pharmaceutical grade Epsom salts, so the water is super dense like at the Dead Sea, allowing you to float on the surface without any strain or effort. You just need to shower with our special organic cleanser, then slip into the tank nude. I'm sorry I'll have to miss that."

Her comment startled me out of my rising fear, and I smirked at her, happy to be distracted a moment from my rising panic. Pri had been bothering me for weeks to stop by her new job and give it a go. She'd gone on and on about how it would be good for a student athlete like me. I didn't believe in any of her new age mumbo jumbo, but I missed her. I wanted to see her again. But it was now clear that I would be seeing basically nothing for the next half hour or so.

"You'll close the hatch behind you with a simple press of this button," Pri went on. "Then you just climb on in and get comfortable. Now, because the temperature of the water is the same as the temperature of your skin, eventually, you'll lose sensation of where your body stops and where the water begins. It's so trippy and amazing. If you're lucky and able to relax enough, you can even experience lucid dreaming, though that's rare on the first float."

"You gotta know that this all sounds like hokey hippie crap," I blurted as my palms started to sweat.

"It's scientifically proven, Jess. There are—"

"Yeah, yeah. You already have me here. I signed your stupid waiver. What else do I need to know?" I didn't mean to be so harsh, but I was tense.

"Well, I know you get claustrophobic sometimes—no, no, it's okay to admit when you're afraid of something, Jess."

"I know that," I insisted angrily, "but I'm not claustrophobic." *I am totally claustrophobic.*

"Jess, why is it so hard for you to admit when you're afraid? It's normal."

"It's not hard to admit because it's not true. I'm not afraid," I lied, planting my feet apart and faking easy confidence. "Just tell me what else I need to know."

"Fine." Pri sighed. "You need to know that in the unlikely event that you do get completely uncharacteristically claustrophobic"—here she inserted a sharp eye roll—"you can hit the panic button on the right-hand side of the tank. It opens up the channel for me to communicate with you. Then if you just need to hear someone's voice to calm you down or ask a question, we can talk, and you'll hear me through the ear plugs because the volume's super loud. Or if you're really panicking, I will help you out of the tank."

Pri came close and grabbed my hands. Heat rushed through me.

"Jess, this is going to be amazing. Just relax and trust it. It can super powerful if you don't fight it. And I'll be just a button push away if you need me. I'm so proud of you for trying this. I know you make fun of all my alternative healing interests, so it really means something to me that you're willing to try this."

Fuck. Here we go again. You sucker.

Pri leaned in and kissed me lightly on the cheek. She smelled like sandalwood, earthy and feminine. I tried to pull her in to a more intimate embrace, but she giggled and resisted.

"You're so bad," she said. It was without real criticism, but she nonetheless added distance between us, removing her hands from my grasp. "Enjoy, Jess. Trust. Let go. I'll see you in ninety minutes."

"What?" I was pretty sure I squeaked. Like a little girl.

"Ninety minutes. Didn't you listen when I was explaining the protocol?"

"Sure. Yes, of course. I just didn't…yeah," I finished lamely, resigned to finding myself in yet another hellish situation at the hands of a beautiful woman. "How will I know when the time is up?" I might have whined.

"Light will start to appear, very gently at first, and then the tank will brighten by degrees. We can set it to any color. But I chose purple for you," she added slyly.

Bitch. I went crazy for Pri's purple-tinged labia when I first went down on her. I'd never dated a person of color before, and porn isn't really my thing, so I had no clue that lips could be purple. It became an inside joke between us. My new favorite color. So obviously she'd torture me with it now.

"See you on the other side, Jessica Martin."

Of course, she left me with that. She knew I hated

being called by my full name. I started to suspect that she'd concocted this whole thing as an elaborate revenge. For what? She left me! Not that that fact was inspiring her to go easy on me. *Fucking women. Can't live with them. Can't live without them. Can't stop finding myself in awkward situations inspired by them.*

With nothing to do but venture forward, I stripped off my clothes and threw them haphazardly on the floor. One step at a time, I told myself, adjusting the water temperature in the shower, then stepping inside. I sniffed the organic all-natural body wash, which smelled of nothing in particular. I lathered it all over, thinking of Pri and how much I wished it was her soaping up all my naughty bits. Pri always went on about my tight, toned body, so I tried to feel myself from her perspective. Running my hands from flat abs to perky tits and strong arms. From my sculpted calves to fuller thighs to the warmth between them. With slippery fingers, I began massaging my clit and thinking of Pri's pretty purple pussy. Well, it was one way to relax before stepping into what felt like a watery coffin. I couldn't climax, though. My mind kept wandering, and my eyes kept returning to the tank.

Let's just get this over with. I stepped carefully onto the rubber mats leading to the tank and popped earplugs into my ears. I pushed the open button, and the egg seemed to hatch, opening smoothly, with an eerie purple glow emanating from its depth. I felt like the doomed, overly trusting astronaut in some space thriller, the one about to go to cryogenic sleep or some such science-y shit in order to withstand space travel. Unbeknownst to her, but super beknownst to the audience, it will not a smooth passage. This was where my brain was as I maneuvered into the mouth of the tank and tried to relax into lying down. So much easier said than done. I consciously breathed long, slow breaths. I tried to think of calming things. Campfires. Sunsets. Jiggling boobs. That kind of thing.

Knowing that I would never really relax into this, I just

went for it and pushed the close button. The door closed with the same slow, eerie motion, the lights dimmed, and I was alone in the dark. In a confined space. All alone. In silence. No big deal, I lied to myself.

I adjusted my position a few times until I found something comfortable. My hands behind my head with my fingers laced behind my neck seemed to be the best. It gave me the illusion of ease and power that I needed. I moved around a bit to explore the limits, made sure I located each surface. And the panic button, obviously.

I waited. Waited…

Ninety freaking minutes. How was I ever going to get through this? I was already antsy. Bored. Anxious. What to do to pass the time? My thoughts raced. My mind wandered to Pri again: the reason I was in this ludicrous situation.

Everything about her was ludicrous. Telling me she couldn't be my girlfriend anymore because she was into "relationship anarchy" now. What the actual fuck? I always felt like a moron with her, secretly trying to catch up, always mentally taking note of obscure new words she'd throw around casually like everyone should know them.

"DIY relationships," she'd explained. "It's like polyamory on speed. It's all about dismantling monogamist privilege. Stepping off the relationship escalator, you know?" *Uh…no, I don't. Come again?*

From what I could glean from her rambling and Google, she meant that she wanted to fuck around. And worse, love around. Play the field sexually and emotionally. I wasn't down with that. Then we started this ridiculous texting war. She'd send me pro-poly quotes about freedom in love. Quotes from some famous Vietnamese monk saying, "You must love in such a way that the person you love feels free." I'd seethe and send back a retaliation quote from the Good Book: "Use your freedom to serve one another in love," Galatians 5:13. It never did any good; she would not be deterred. She just replied with some Indian poet's bullshit words: "Love does not claim possession but gives freedom." Well, I wouldn't be deterred either. I met her poet with a songwriter and raised her one level of cynicism: "Freedom's just another word for nothing left to lose." This was how we always rolled: Bicker. Banter. Fuck. Repeat.

Why were women so infuriating? Why did I always find myself in these dumbass situations trying to please them? For someone who hated giving up control, I sure as hell found myself doing it enough. I seethed. So much for relaxing. Floating in a dull bubble of nothing interesting, I was left alone with just my thoughts, and they were pissed. Pissed at how the women I liked were always so difficult and demanding. I shook my head slightly and realized with a start that I didn't know if my eyes were open or closed. I blinked consciously and realized I couldn't tell the difference. How long had I been in here? Floating in this weird womb tomb space bubble.

To pass the time with more pleasant thoughts, I start doing the lesbian version of counting sheep, trying to recall all my prior lovers' breasts with perfect photographic precision. I was mid-list when Pri's voice filled the void I was floating in, disrupting my reverie.

"How are you doing in there, Jess?"

"Whoa, Pri. How long have I been in here? Is the time almost up?"

"Hardly. I just wanted to check in. You okay?"

"I'm fine."

"You sure?"

"Yes, *I'm fine*," I answered tartly, annoyed with her obvious worry as well as her avoidance of my question about the time.

"Okay, then I'm going to read to you for a bit. This isn't usually part of the protocol, of course, but since you're a VIP, you get extra-special treatment. I scheduled you for the last float of the night for a reason. Even sent Jason home early. So now it's just you and me. And some sexy French poetry. Sound intriguing?"

I squirmed in my holding tank, unable to say anything coherent. Pri spoke four languages. I used to like watching the shifting shapes of her mouth as she read to me in a foreign tongue, my head cradled in her lap, snuggling in her tiny apartment bedroom. She started reciting.

Fuck. She sounded so sexy when she spoke in French. I never knew what she was saying, but hell, half the time, I didn't know what she was talking about when she spoke in English. It was such a musical language, and I just let myself get lost in its melodic sounds.

As she spoke such beautiful, unintelligible words, visions of bodies embracing rose in my mind. Visions of lovers past. Their blessed beauty. Filling up my mind. This one's shoulder blades. The curve of that one's hips. So many women. Merging. Loving. Blending in rhythm with Pri's sounds.

The cadence and lilt of her voice danced through my head. It felt like it went on for hours. It caressed my skin, washed over my surfaces, and floated away beyond. I had the impression of free floating in space. Moving further and further from myself and yet somehow deeper and deeper into myself. Warmth spread through me, and the warmth held color. I saw streaks of shifting color intertwine and undulate inside me. An aurora borealis of self. The lights blazed along my limbs and lit up the night sky that was both me and not me. Cosmic colors flared. Ethereal shades ablaze. I was…I was…having some kind of bizarre whole-body spasm, I realized, laughing for no reason.

"Jess? Jess? You okay?"

The laughter wouldn't stop; it poured and poured out of me. My whole body vibrated with it. I realized with a start that I was coming. In a thrilling new way I'd never experienced before. Every part of my body sang with delight. Everywhere that was me was thrumming with profound satisfaction. But I hadn't even touched myself. Or had I? I'd lost all sense of myself before the orgasm had me come rushing back into my flesh. What the fuck?

"Jess?"

"Yeah, yeah, sorry. I don't know what just happened." I gasped.

"Were you lucid dreaming? Did you see things?"

"Maybe. I don't know. Yeah, I guess so."

"Jess, that's amazing. Did you see sexy things? Did you dream of me?" she asked teasingly. "Because those poems were hot. I have my tits out. Sitting right here at the reception desk with no shirt on. Anyone walking by could see."

"Pri!"

"What? It's after nine o'clock on a Tuesday night. Who's gonna be walking by the strip mall at this time of night? I couldn't help myself. I was playing with my tits the whole time and wishing you were doing it instead."

I was pretty sure an animal growling sound escaped my throat.

"Anyway, if you want to fuck me one more time, you have exactly one minute before I put these tits away for the night. Hope you're not too disoriented." She laughed. "Fifty-nine, fifty-eight, fifty-seven, fifty-six…"

What? Fuck! I fumbled to find the open button and cursed the slow pace of the hydraulic arms. The light in the room was blinding. My legs shook, and I felt unsteady, but somehow, I awkwardly managed to flounder out of the tank and upright onto the rubber mats.

"Forty-five, forty-four, forty-three…Don't slip getting to me. Forty-two, forty-one…"

A towel? My clothes? No time. I oriented myself in the room and made for the door on wobbly legs. My head was spinning, and I felt like I was moving underwater. But there was a gorgeous woman awaiting my skills, and I would not disappoint or miss out, goddammit. I lurched down the hall buck naked and disheveled but determined.

I rounded the corner to the front reception, and Pri had not lied. She was sitting at the welcome desk playing with her nipples in full view of the giant storefront windows. Her eyes widened and began twinkling as soon as she saw me, no doubt looking ridiculous, wet and disoriented from the float tank. She began to laugh, and it infuriated me. I broke the space between us in a few purposeful strides and suppressed her laughter with a forceful kiss, pulling her to her feet and pinning her against the desk with the full length of my body. I kissed my way down her neck and shoulder to her chest. Sucked hard on her right nipple while my hand kneaded her left breast.

She started yammering something. I removed my hand from her breast and placed it over her mouth. She protested vigorously, so I removed it and stood to face her. Waited. Impatient. Breathing heavily.

"What happened in the tank, Jess? You look crazy intense. Did you have visions or something?"

I closed my eyes and took a deep, calming breath. "Priyanka Patel, I am going to fuck you now, and for once in your goddamn life, you are going to shut the fuck up and stop questioning everything." Her eyes lit up, and I knew she was into it. With that, I forced my hands under her skirt and yanked off her pink lace panties. Pushed her back on the desk. Scooted her just where I needed her and buried my face in her pretty purple pussy.

She tasted as good as I remembered. Sweeter perhaps for the time elapsed since she had last cradled my face between her lean brown thighs. Her hips moved just as I remembered. Her sounds, their beloved range of reaction, were all so familiar. This was where I wanted to be. Now and always. Now and always. Loving this crazy, flaky, wicked smart and sexy woman.

Now and always.

Craving her kiss, I moved to press her lips to mine,

and she burst out laughing. Big, mood-crashing, full-bellied laughs that seemed to come from nowhere. I froze, confused. Pri went on laughing, struggling to stop long enough to explain, then cracking up and failing to explain this newfound awkwardness. I got paranoid and looked down at myself to see what the hell was so funny. That was when I saw that I was alarmingly white, covered in a film of salt residue. Indeed, I looked ridiculous. And now that I was paying attention, my skin was stinging and itchy. Guess it was important to rinse off. Pri went on laughing, and it irritated me more than the salt.

"Yes, yes, it's funny. You're so funny, Pri. The things you get me to do for you. Just hilarious."

"It is," she managed, wiping a tear from her eyes.

"Very clever, Pri. Bet you knew I'd look like this, huh?" Pri was overcome with another giggle fit and hid her face in her hands, confirming my suspicions.

"Yep. Funny. So very funny," I said.

I twirled her around forcefully so that she was bent over the desk. Kicked her feet apart. Pressed into her. I looked around for some item to use as punishment, but there was nary a ruler to be found in this office. I improvised and grabbed the iPad they used to have clients sign in. "I'm gonna fuck you now just the way you like it best, but there's a catch. You're going to read me this never-ending waiver that you make everybody sign. And every time that you fuck something up, I'm gonna punish you. Every time you pause too long or stumble over a word or make any noise at all that is not related to the letters on that document, you can expect a repercussion. Do you understand?" She moaned and wiggled her ass, showing me how much she thrilled to these moments when I took charge. As usual, it emboldened me. "It's got some pretty big legal words in it, but you're so clever, it shouldn't be a problem for you, right Pri? Little Miss Fucking Know-It-All?"

I pulled up the waiver and placed the iPad before her

face. "Put your hands behind your head. Lace your fingers together and just keep them there. Don't fucking move from this position. Got it?"

I stepped away from her then to admire how she was spread out on the desk. Long legs wide apart, ass and just a hint of pussy showing, skirt hiked up to her hips. She looked mildly uncomfortable leaning over the desk with her hands supporting her neck. I liked that nothing held her there but my commands. I could put her in awkward positions too. "Start reading, smart girl…go on, read for me. Tell me all about your liquid torture chamber." Pri laughed, and I smacked her ass hard and swift with my open palm. "Did I say something funny?"

"No."

"Good, then get to work."

Pri began reading the waiver in a strange, excited voice. I let her ramble for a bit without touching her.

"I, the undersigned, absolve Aqua Wellness and their employees from any and all liability in connection with…"

I crouched down and began kissing, licking and nibbling my way up her legs. I paused at the backs of her knees. Flicked my tongue ever so lightly right where I knew she was most ticklish. As predicted, she stumbled. *Smack!* She yelped, and I smacked her ass again. "You can do better than that. Come on, Pri."

She rallied and began enunciating the words with exaggerated precision and focus. I returned to my journey up her legs, worshipping the backs of her thighs this time. As I approached her ass, she couldn't keep from squirming, and I smiled to myself, pleased with how we responded to each other so naturally. I trailed my tongue all along the curve of her bottom, interspersing kisses along the trail. Then bit down. She jumped and shrieked in surprise. I feigned disappointment in her dereliction of duty and doled out the appropriate punishment in response. This went on for some time with slight variations, but always the same pattern: tease, provoke, then punish.

Eventually, she abandoned the pretense of reading aloud. She was too far gone for that. As we both craved, my fingers found their way between her legs. Like I said: Tease. Provoke. Punish. Repeat. I massaged her vulva in maddening slow circles. Never giving her what she wanted. Making her wait for it. "You don't miss me at all, do you?"

"Not really," she lied, just to be a brat.

Leaning over her, putting my weight on the full length of her, I whispered in her ear, "No, not at all. I can tell by the way your pussy is so wet." She continued to squirm and push up against my hand, urging me on. "No, you want to be free. You want to play around. You don't miss me at all. Just like you didn't miss me on your birthday when you drunk-dialed me and begged me to come over and give you birthday spankings. Just like you didn't miss me last month when I met you at the park at midnight and finger-fucked you in the gazebo." I started to circle her clit now, priming her for my fingers. I felt her start to tremble and backed off, unwilling to release her so speedily.

"Turn around and face me when I'm talking to you." Pri extricated herself from her prior position and turned, her face a mixture of eager desire and impish mischief. I wrapped my fist in her hair and pulled her into me again. Exploring her mouth with a wild tongue. Breathing hard. I broke away and gazed in her eyes. "You arranged all this, huh? Making sure you were the last one locking up? Bringing along a book of French poetry to read to me to get me all worked up?" We kissed again, and I nibbled her lip. "Yeah, totally not the behavior of an ex desperate for another go." I smirked and held her gaze. "You fucking need me. You want me to admit my fears, but you can't even admit your desires. Tell me you want me.

Tell me you need my fingers in your cunt." I slapped her face lightly, the way she liked it, with just enough force to excite her. "Tell me." I tightened my grip on her hair.

"I don't mind your fingers in my cunt from time to time," she drawled, smiling.

Fuck, she was infuriating. "Oh, you don't mind. You don't mind? That's great. Do you mind this?" I asked, thrusting two fingers into her pussy and pumping away without build-up, pulling her hair and biting her earlobe. "Do you fucking mind this?" I said with a growl, removing my fingers long enough to slap her pussy a few times. "Is this okay once in a while?"

Her moans answered for her, and I gave her what we both wanted, filling her with my fingers and fury and lust. She locked her eyes on mine and started screaming the yes, yes, yes that always signaled her climax, a sound I sought out with ludicrous dedication. I'd go to any lengths. Do anything. Face any discomfort to hear that yes, yes, yes burst from those pretty purple lips. As it did. Yet again.

"Yes. Yes. Yes!"

Pri collapsed in my arms, and I held her close, reveling in the scents and sounds of her. My on-again, off-again girlfriend who I could never understand except in the bedroom. I buried my face in her hair and just breathed, wishing this moment of intimate connection would never end. That we could stay in this feeling forever. But Pri was never mushy like me after sex. There was never pillow talk and cuddles. She recovered all too quickly, straightened up, and started looking for her clothes. I just watched, forlorn with the dread of disconnecting again.

"Wow, that was amazing, Jess. Mary's gonna love tonight's security vid."

"What?" I shrieked. "You better be fucking joking," I said, scanning the ceiling for cameras. "Pri!"

"What? They won't be able to ID you."

I started pacing and looking for something to throw on. "That's not the fucking point, Pri. It would have been nice to know." Pri pointed to a closet, and I found freshly laundered towels. I hastily wrapped one around my salt-encrusted body. "Oh my God, Pri. You'll totally lose your job."

"I was leaving anyway. Now they'll have something fun to remember me by. I'll be that crazy chick who went out with a bang," she said, laughing to herself.

"Wait, what?" I replied, struggling to keep up. "You're quitting? You just got this job."

"I know. But I'm not feeling it anymore."

"Of course," I said, rolling my eyes, unaccountably angry again. "You never stick to anything." Okay, maybe accountably angry. At her for not sticking with me.

"I don't know," Pri cooed, sidling up to me flirtatiously. "Seems like I'm pretty stuck to you." She petted my hair and face teasingly.

"You're not...argh, you're fucking impossible."

"And adorable and quirky and sexy and super smart and—"

"Humble. Very humble."

"Yep, that too." She kissed me super gently, super sweetly.

"What am I going to do with you?" I asked seriously.

"Hopefully very bad things," Pri said, eyes a-twinkle.

"Pri, seriously, we can't keep doing this."

"Why not? You can't tell me you didn't have fun tonight. You'll be eighty years old on your deathbed with dentures and cataracts and smile to yourself remembering this epic fuck. That's what I want: to be *unforgettable*." She gave one of her characteristic, melodramatic gestures of excitement mentioned earlier.

"Then stay with me and make memories with me," I said shamelessly.

She held my head and studied me in silence. There was a pause full of everything unsaid between us. Finally, she whispered, "It's not what I want. And it's not who I am."

Belong to me. Be mine, I wanted to scream. Instead, I

buried my face in her hair again, pulling her close one more time. This infuriating woman I couldn't live with or without. On and on we went, fucking and fighting, fighting and fucking. Bicker. Banter. Couldn't be together. Couldn't be apart.

"Maybe we should talk to a counselor or something," I said desperately. "See if there's some way to compromise. I know you love me, and I love you too. This is crazy!"

"What compromise, Jess? You can't be kind of free. I'm a free spirit. You know that. It's what you love about me even as you hate it. If you're not willing to explore a more open-minded concept of love with me, then we can't realistically be together except in this tortured sort of way we keep coming back to. Besides, I'm leaving with Grace on Friday to go backpacking through Central America for three months. You remember Grace, right? My yoga instructor? Well, she was supposed to be going with her boyfriend but…"

Pri's voice continued as she went about closing up the spa, casually, like nothing had just happened, like we hadn't just had an epic experience together, like she hadn't just uprooted my world once again. I watched her go about the mundane tasks of closing up, chattering on, oblivious while I stood rooted to the spot, something momentous but unclear shifting inside of me.

I realized she was staring at me and had stopped talking.

"Are you listening? You should go wash off. We need to go."

I turned robotically and headed back to the liquid torture chamber, where I turned on the shower and stood under it unmoving, just letting its spray rain down on my flesh unimpeded. I felt…like I should be raging. Or crying. My go-to reactions to Pri's impossible personality. But I didn't really feel like doing either.

Pri had shown herself to me time and time again. This wasn't new. This was who she was. And truthfully, I loved her for it, not despite it. *I don't know why I always choose women like her. But I am the one doing the choosing.* Was there part of me that enjoyed being bound and tortured in this way? Did I think that was all I deserved? Should I have been seeking out another kind of connection? Was that even possible for me, or would I be bored with a nice girl who returned my affection faithfully and conventionally?

My gaze wandered to the float tank, hatch open, opposite me. My time within it struck me as a bizarre microcosm of my entire experience with Pri because for all that it tested and irritated me, it also gave me the most ecstatic and unique high of my life. What a weird little egg it was. Incubating strange truths. But what was the truth? After my time inside, who did I want to emerge as?

Did I want a traditional, merry-go-round life with a sweet girl who would meet my needs?

Or did I need some level of passionate, roller-coaster intensity that only a bad girl could provide?

Was there another option I couldn't yet see?

Evidently, I had three months to find out.

PART FIVE: EARTH. AIR. FIRE. WATER.
ELEMENTAL EROTICA

EARTH

Lover,

The last time I put pen to paper in love for you, we were still a thrilling mystery to each other. Do you remember the insistence of our desire? How I stripped you naked again and again, ever hungry for the core of you to be revealed? All these years later, I still long to strip you naked, the urge still strong to seek out what is now the sweet familiarity of you. There is always more to discover in the depths of you. Thank you for that.

I know you are at work right now. Busy doing your small but essential part to change the world. Bringing home the tofu and the kitty treats, as we always said. I can see you going about your business day in your well-pressed clothes, your shiny shoes and expensive watch, your sexy professional aura that is so well known to me. You do not know that I pen these lines, naked and freshly bathed, lounging upon our huge bed. I will mail this when I am done, and it will be another of my unexpected gifts. A memory of our loving we will reread when we can be together, naked and freshly bathed, in our huge bed.

I didn't intend to write you a love letter. I had the day off today. Went for a bike ride through the trails. Flew through the dappling forest light, my body soaked in sweat, my muscles alive and burning, and my mouth stuck in a silly grin despite the threat of swallowing bugs. I went for a quick refreshing dip and then came home to putter about our garden, both relaxed and invigorated.

That was when I thought of you. The sun warm on the back of my neck, my fingers full of the earth, crouching amidst all the greenery, I had this fantasy that you had come home early to surprise me. I giggled out loud to myself alone in the backyard, I was so convinced. I could almost feel your hands reaching around me from behind and grabbing at my breasts, free and full beneath my white tank top.

"I missed you." You growled in my ear, fairly crushing my breasts against my chest as you hunkered down beside me and licked the sun's warmth from my neck. I'm sure I must've looked ridiculous if anyone could've seen me, eyes closed, spade poised in midair as I imagined you tugging at my clothes, impatient for my flesh right there in the backyard.

"Wait," I whispered, untucking the shirt carefully from my shorts and raising my arms high above my head. I looked back and smiled slyly. "Okay." You slipped it gingerly over my head and moaned, running your open palms along my outstretched arms and torso. I reached back and grabbed the back of your head, pulling you closer as your hands reached for my chest again and your breath warmed my ear.

"I hate being away from you," you whispered in a low voice, wrapping your arms around my waist in a full embrace and pulling me tight against you. You leaned back with me, and I laughed, fearful of you losing your balance and me tumbling back onto you.

"Careful," I said, and disentangling myself, I turned to you slowly, aware of the power of my half-naked self, of the effect that seeing me outside and topless would evoke in you. I watched your eyes widen, your breath catch, and your eyebrows come together with determination as you sought me out again. But I wanted to see you resplendently bare as well, and so it was off with the tidy work shirt, off with the sports bra, and there we were, kneeling in the grass, oblivious and turned on in the mid-afternoon sun, your carefully tended clothes crumpled and forgotten in the dirt.

The tips of our breasts just kissing, I looked deep into your eyes and watched them light up, the corners of your eyelids crinkling. I matched my breathing to yours, slowed down the world, and rested for a moment in the safety of your gaze. You leaned forward then and touched your lips to mine, gently and with much held back. I smiled through the kiss and wrapped my arms around your broad shoulders, trailed my fingernails along your back.

"Make love to me in our garden?" I asked simply.

"You don't have to ask me twice," you answered and laid me softly upon the lawn. You kissed your way down my body and removed the last pieces of clothing separating my skin from your touch. You looked up then and scanned the boundaries of our yard, cautious. I craned my neck and looked too. We were safe. We both laughed.

"We are very naughty girls, aren't we?" I said, laughter still bubbling in my throat.

"Mm-hmm," you murmured, looking down at me intently. The laughter evaporated in my mouth; your eyes were so full of fire, and the ache between my legs rose. I rocked slightly, side to side, nursing the need. I closed my eyes to better feel the old sensation of wanting you. Stems of grass tickled the soles of my feet. Insects hummed nearby. A breeze blew the scent of lavender to my nostrils. I pressed my knees together tightly, trying to contain the growing urge.

Your hand came then, firm and pulsing upon my thigh. Next came the words we always used, a sultry invitation, cooed into my ear. "Are you going to open for me, baby?" The moment of *yes*, as I relinquished control, handed my need over to you. How I cherish the much-loved, time-worn ritual of you parting my legs, that moment a rushing, stand-still climax of its own.

Every time, the approach seems new. Today, your fingers

slid maddening slow to the center of my desire. "*Please.*" I had no patience. No ability to savor the suspense. I thrust my hips skyward, and you chuckled low and soft in the back of your throat. But you gave me what I wanted. Following my rhythm this time, you touched me right away, and I was already in flood. Warm and expecting you. A space of intimate welcome.

How much detail do you need, my love? You know the contours of our lovemaking already. I asked for more and more, and you kept giving. Your tongue spelled out the sublime like a secret language upon my lips, and still I wanted more. Like when we were young and everything about our lives was utterly urgent, intense, all-consuming. There was only ever *this* and nothing else. You filled me to overflowing, and still it was not enough. I wanted you to pour from me, burst forth like lava, hot and wild.

We came together to the precipice, the space of trust where I had to slow down, take a breath, lock eyes with you, and open myself beyond what felt possible. Your eyes were always so concerned here, your movements so careful and subtle. It always got to me. "Keep going," I said, amazed at my own capacity to hold you, and when at last, *at last*, your entire hand was swallowed up by me, I was in such awe. As full up as you were terrified and exhilarated. You were entirely inside me, a visible symbol of our desire, patience, and faith. We stayed a moment in this victory, but then some slight twitch, any small movement of yours ignited me again, and I was so full, so entirely *full* with you, that there was no room in me for anything but pleasure. No space for self-consciousness, no room for doubt or thought or any emotion other than the excruciating totality of us. Just us...

So that, my love, is how I spent my afternoon. Dreaming of you and the love that we've nurtured. It's a lush and abundant space just like our garden. I don't know what it is about being outside with grit beneath my nails, but it's always oddly pleased me. The sensuality and groundedness of it, I guess.

Even when I was a kid, I used to love to bask in the summer sun, my fingers deftly arranging the sand in my sandbox to fit the shapes of my imagination. I always had sand in my hair, between my toes, everywhere. Drove my poor mother nuts.

Well, darling, this letter is getting pretty long, and I'm starting to get off topic, so I should finish it up, seal it, and send it off through the post to end up a surprise in our mailbox for you a few days from now. I should get up now, dress, and make some dinner for us. Prepare to greet you at the door. But it would be so much more satisfying to remain here and think of you. To greet you naked and hungry at the door. To pull you into the kitchen without a word and take my fill of you. Leave you shaking and sated on the floor, and then just feed you whatever is within arm's reach in the refrigerator once I'm done with you.

Perhaps I could lead you upstairs and pull out the strap-on. Feel the leather slide up my thighs and the cold of the metal on my skin as you adjust the buckles. You know how this story would go, don't you? The big tease. The drawn-out preliminaries. The twinkling in my eyes. Would I coo to you too? "Are you going to open for me, baby?" And would you open? Would you take as much as I could give you? Could we reach a point where you would be ready to receive me? Where you could climb on top of me unabashed and take your pleasure wholeheartedly, your breasts two ripe promises dancing before my eager lips? My thighs would hold you, my hips would angle just so, my lips would form your name, and you could erupt, as I had dreamed earlier, a mountain of flesh bucking violently above me. An earthquake of great proportions. Seismic tremors.

Hurry home…

Love,

Your Girl

AIR

"Strip."

You laugh and try to lift up my dress, but I stop you. "No. You. Strip naked." I'm staring into you, and it feels deliciously familiar. You decide not to be shy and begin to undress, meeting my eyes, maintaining the challenge. You finish and stand there firmly. Proud. I turn my back and light a candle. I hold a stick of incense in its flame until it catches fire. I watch it burn a moment, then open my lips and blow. Scented wisps of smoke rise in a spiraling column from the stick. I can feel your eyes, patient and expectant, on my back. I place the incense in its holder and move to the stereo. I can hear you shift your stance. "Lay on the bed," I say, perusing my playlists. I can feel your cocky smirk from here. I play some jazz quietly and turn to find you kneeling on the bed with my black silk scarf wrapped around your wrists and your eyebrows raised high.

"What's this for, baby?"

"To put you in your place, of course," I answer, unwrapping the scarf from where you wound it round your wrists and tying it instead as a blindfold around your head. "Mmm." You're smiling, and I push you down on the bed. "Where's the feather I gave you?"

"Right where you told me to keep it."

I smile and brush my lips against your forehead as I scramble off the bed and search your inner jacket pocket for the feather. It's there. Gleaming purple black. I finger its shape and then return to you. I trace the outline of your body slowly with the feather. "Do you remember when we found this?" I let the question trail through your mind like the feather does your body. Your lips upturn but do not open. "Maybe this will remind you," I say, throwing open the window. The cold of winter rushes into our bedroom.

"Shit! Yes, I remember. I remembered all along. Just close the window. It's freezing," you say, trying to grab at the blanket for warmth.

I stop your hands with mine. "When I ask you a question, I expect an answer." My body is draped over yours, and I know you don't want me to move, so I make sure I do. I close the window only slightly and lean over to put my lips but not my body close to your ear. "Be good," I whisper. "And I'll warm you up. But first I'm gonna make you suffer. If that's all right with you." I wait for the yield of your nod and brush my breasts against your arm as I lean in to add, "I'm going to leave you for a while because I have to get something, but I want you to stay right here in the cold, just waiting and wanting. I want you to concentrate on how the cool air feels blowing across your body, and I want you to remember the last time you felt this cold and turned on at the same time. Remember… at the cabin…on the snowmobile…in the ice-fishing hut," and at this, I laugh, and you squirm, and I get up and leave.

Your nipples are tight, and you give a little involuntary shudder. The room is chilly but not unbearable, especially not in this state. The occasional blast of cold from the window is just bordering on the edge of unpleasant but is never quite that bad. You imagine me walking down the stairs, my ass swinging pleasantly in my turquoise dress, the one that shows off my legs so well you always beg me to wear it.

And today I did. Surprised you at the office with some lunch, packed very sweetly in a brown paper bag with a little red heart on it. I kissed you on the cheek, handing it to you, and the smell of my perfume and my hair, combined with the unexpected pleasure of seeing me at work looking so beautiful, sent a shot of desire straight through you. You tried to convince me to let you take me home and take *me* over your lunch break. I laughed coyly and said I'd see you later tonight, turning and leaving you wanting. You sat at your desk frustrated and fantasizing until hunger got the best of you, and you opened my package.

Inside was one of your favorite dishes along with one solitary toasted marshmallow and an envelope. Your brows knitted together in curiosity over the marshmallow. You opened the envelope for an answer. Inside was a feather, *the* feather, huge and black, as stark against the white envelope as it had been against the white of the snow when we first saw it. I had brought it home, cleaned it, and kept it as a souvenir of that time. You twirled it between your fingers and let your mind wander…and then the marshmallow made sense. Of course. The fire we'd made on the side of the snowmobile trail. We'd roasted marshmallows in the middle of the bush, but how did I roast a marshmallow now? With a candle? You laughed out loud at the image and searched the envelope. Inside was a note saying I had a surprise or two planned for you to bring some cheer to this dreary February. I knew a girl who grew up on an island needed sunshine, and I planned to deliver. You closed your eyes and imagined…

Work dragged on interminably, until at last you were free, and you practically ran out the door to your car, and then you stopped abruptly. I was there. Leaning against your car, smiling. Happy and confused, you rushed over to hug me.

"Where's the feather?" I asked. You patted your suit jacket, and I smiled. "Keep it there."

"What's going on?"

"We're going out for dinner," I said, and we did. A long and scrumptious form of foreplay. You harassed me all through the meal, and I deferred your questions until we got home, and you saw the bedroom where most of the questions were immediately answered. The sex lights were on. There was a Crock-Pot set up by the bed along with a towel and some Kama Sutra oil. And draped casually across the foot of the bed, a black silk scarf…

Now the door opens slowly. "Did you miss me?"

A long, drawn-out "Yes" is your response.

I approach the bed and climb on top of you, straddling your chest with my legs. "Open your mouth." You obey, and a perfect drop of ice-cold water hits your lower lip and then your tongue. You moan and eagerly take the drops falling from my hand. I am holding the ice cube tight, enthralled with how it drips down my thumb, hovers there a moment on the tip, and then free falls into your awaiting mouth. The drops are sudden, localized points of chill, and yet somehow, they inspire heat. The blood in your vulva, in your fingers, in your brain, pulsing. I make it a little messy so you can't get every drop. I watch the water trail down from the corner of your lips down your neck. I watch, and I talk, my breath warm on your ear. "Cold, baby, huh? Just like the time…you know…just like then." Your mouth is so eager. I start to dribble it on your collarbone, your neck, the slopes of your breasts. Your breath catches. "Don't worry, baby. I'm not going to let you freeze." My lips find every drop, warm each spot with my heat.

I grab another ice cube and touch it to your lips, trace them and whisper, "I want your body to remember, with your mind, with my words." You're squirming and pawing at me, but I grab your arms and put them straight out at your sides.

"Now, listen close, honey. I have a challenge for you," I say, placing an ice cube in both of your palms and closing your fingers over them. "If you can hold on to these without letting go until they melt, I'll give you the *best damn lesbian blow-job you've ever had*."

You give a low laugh full of grit and desire and clench your fists. I grab another cube of ice and continue to tease you with it, taking my time. Your body is shaking, determined. I trickle a freezing rainfall upon your nipples. I see how far up I can hold the cube and still hit the tight tip that is my target. Every time a drop falls, you tremble a little, and I reward you with a press of my lips. Down your stomach, past your belly button, down to there...there.

"Fuck!" You jerk as the drop hits your clit, and your hands open a moment but quickly close again.

"Don't lose now, honey. Not when you're so close." I laugh and move down along your body, trailing my breath, hot between your legs. I kiss you gently, as I have been with every drop, and you moan lightly. I give tentative, short flicks with my tongue, warming you slowly, never giving quite enough, that is, until I *do*, and it's sizzling, and we are crazed and noisy, unmindful of the open window. I lose all memory of the game that we are playing, of the purpose of this evening, of everything except the sensation of your desire under my mouth, greedy and sweet. So sweet. So warm. So *cold*?

"Ha," you yell, clapping your frozen, wet hands hard on my ass under my dress. "I win. You owe me."

"Whatever. I didn't say you could freeze *me*."

"Didn't say I couldn't either, now pay up, girlfriend!" You chuckle, your face one big smirk.

"You're lucky I'm a woman of my word," I say, but I'm smiling, happy our sex life is always so playful, unpredictable. I maneuver my body so that I'm straddling your leg, and I take your poor chilly fingers in my own. I open them and place a kiss in the center of your palm. I start to tickle it with my tongue and then slide my tongue up to the tip of your longest finger. I begin to nibble, suck, lick, bite, tap, brush, and tantalize your fingers with my mouth. We both begin to gyrate, and I begin to talk again, asking you if you remember the last time that your fingers were this cold.

I am wearing silk panties under my dress, and I move them aside periodically with my gyration so you can feel my wetness on your thigh. Just for a moment and then it's the soft slipperiness of silk again. You keep trying to raise your thigh higher so I can grind into you more intensely, and you grab at me, trying to slip your fingers under my panties, but I slap your hand and tell you to be patient.

You grab my ass instead and try for my breasts, but my dress is in the way, and you growl "Take it off," but I won't. I go on moving my hips in rhythm with my own yearning and continue telling you the story whenever my mouth is free for a moment.

"Do you remember the snowmobile?"

I remember. Massive steel vibrating between the grip of our thighs, the speed and the wind flushing us with exhilaration. How we saw wild deer, curious yet furtive in the woods. How we swigged whiskey from a flask like real rednecks and learned to love the burning slide of it down our throats. The smell of a woodstove burning in our little cabin. The rage of a winter snow squall. The quiet joy of drinking our morning tea and watching monster snowflakes the size of cotton balls plunk against the windowpanes. Daring to snuggle naked under two huge duvets. And then there was the time we discovered the crow's feather. Striking and magical, stuck in the snow just outside the ice fishing hut. We hadn't noticed it before we went in, so it seemed almost a cosmic wink from the universe after…well…

We threw off our helmets, stumbling, laughing, shaking out our hair, cheeks red and eyes bright. We let ourselves right into the vacant hut. Trespassed. Entered the forbidden. You pushed me rough against the rickety wooden walls, and I was afraid the whole structure would tumble, but it didn't, and you didn't seem like you would've cared anyway. You were intent, focused. I couldn't stop laughing for the sheer craziness, and you couldn't stop ripping my many layers of clothes aside. I leaned my head against the coarse wooden wall and listened as the wind raced through the cracks as you raced through to me, pain and desire both searing as your fingers found me. The wind was screaming.

"Baby, now. Please. Baby…"

I was so warm and ready, I expected you to melt, but instead, I did.

"Yes."

And we are both coming now, finding our pleasure, and I move my mouth over to your ear so you can hear how satisfied I am.

Yes.

Yes.

We hold each other in the quiet after. Content.

On shaking legs, I disengage from you and sit up to get a good look at your full, sated body. "That was the best damn remedy for frostbite ever, huh?" We both laugh, and I close the window as you remove the blindfold. You grab me in another embrace and devour me with your eyes now that it's permitted. Your hands are brushing my hair as you smile at me, looking right into my eyes, happy.

"Thanks."

"Don't thank me yet. It's not over. I'm just getting *warmed up*." I laugh stupidly at my own joke, and you roll your eyes.

You groan and add, "I can handle the ice torture, but no more of your jokes, okay?"

"Be nice to me," I say. "Or you won't get…*this*!" I twirl around, revealing two smooth gray stones still dripping from the Crock-Pot. "A warmed river stone massage."

"Oh, *yeah*." You're on your stomach without another word, and I'm laughing, moving over to you and placing one in each palm where the ice cubes once were. Their heat warms you, pulsating deep into your flesh. They feel so secure and solid in your hands. I place them one by one, weighty and soothing, in a line down your body. The hollow where your head meets your neck, along your spine, the hill of your ass, along your legs. Each time, I place a kiss there before I place the rock. I tell you why. "This stone is for how you make sure you get one good kiss out of me every day. This stone is for teaching me the importance of looking people in the eye. This stone is for being patient with my need to alphabetize the spices." I trail my nails around the stones, dancing them along your flesh, like ice skating. Your body feels amazingly relaxed, the warmth and the smooth circular weight of the stones working like a sedative. Your breathing is slow and deep, and your grin is uncontrollable.

I've let all the stones impart their heat, and I can tell you're getting far too tranquil, so I smack your butt like you did to me and announce, "And this smack is just because I love ya!"

The sudden smarting sensation rouses you, and you turn over, hungry for my mouth. We kiss long and searching kisses. "Wait. Wait," I say, breaking away despite your groan. I grab the Kama Sutra oil, unscrew the lid, and dip the tips of my fingers inside. I keep my eyes locked with yours and trace along your nipples. "I've warmed you up, but now I've got to get you *hot*, you see."

"I see all right." We both have crooked smiles. I circle you and circle you, then bend down, eyes still locked, to blow. The oil heats up, and you open your mouth and breathe in sharply but do not break my stare. I try again, adding my tongue to the mix this time, and it works. You close your eyes and exhale, moaning. We play awhile this way. Heat and breath. Wetness.

I reach down to find you and discover that your waters run deep. I wish to drown. I start to work on your clit with my tongue. A violent wave rocks your body. I am in ecstasy, totally caught up. The motions are mesmerizing as we rock together. I am so gentle, so light; I am barely there, mostly just my breath, the tip of my tongue just flicking, just tracing you. I see a feather in my mind, fluttering, tumbling from the sky. I feel like it, falling, twirling, dancing with the wind. Everything a wonderfully breezy blur. Your breasts I'm holding tight like handles as we race with the wind, and then I'm warm again, deep inside you, snuggling safe from the storm that rages outside, and we're listening together to the moans of the wind against our shelter. The wind is wild. It's powerful. It sounds like my voice, and it's howling *I want you.*

FIRE

I had the wildest dream...

I am standing naked in a stream, several women's hands upon me. They rub a coarse sweet-smelling balm in circles upon my flesh. They are efficient, solemn. Another woman stands in front of me, a gourd filled with water raised in her arms to shower me. The rays of the setting sun stream through her arms, framing her, inspiring a silent awe in me. She wears an elaborately beaded necklace. Her eyes hold mine with the warmth of familiarity, the look of one who has loved me long. Her eyes are framed with an abundance of furrows.

She pours the water over me, dips the gourd, and pours again. I enjoy the sensation of it streaming down my body. She smiles and looks to the other women. They begin to massage an earthy-scented oil into my skin. I don't understand what is happening. I want to ask the woman with the necklace how she knows me, but I know somehow that the silence we are moving in is sacred. I try to ask her with my eyes. She does not answer. Only looks at me with deep contentment and sincerity of affection. I close my eyes and surrender to the sensation of the hands, firm and earnest upon me.

The elder woman wades to the shore and returns with a necklace as intricately beaded as her own. She ties it around my neck, holding my eyes with her own all the while. I try to understand what she is saying, but I only know that something important will come to be this night. I feel certain that the moon will rise full and powerful this evening and that this bathing and whatever is to follow is somehow connected to the moon's coming into its highest, most potent self.

Strips of cloth are tied to my biceps and thighs. Beadwork of every color covers my neck, wrists, and ankles. I realize I am being ritually adorned. The weight of the jewelry weighs me down, holding me closer to the earth. The woman approaches with a tremendous piece of beadwork. I look closer and realize slowly that it is not made of beading but of bone. A skirt of animal bones. I am afraid of it.

The woman stands before me, so close her toes are touching the tips of mine beneath the water. The skirt looms in the space between us, held out in her arms. She ties it briskly around my waist, her eyes flashing a warning, something significant that I cannot grasp, and I am again frightened. A cloth is tied around my eyes so I cannot even seek hers for solace. My wrists are bound before me, and I am led, uncertain, out of the water.

The bones are hard but smooth, dripping against my legs, stirring in rhythm with my steps as I move along, guided by the older woman. I try to map where she is taking me, for the land feels familiar under my feet, yet I have only the vaguest sense that I have been here before. There are stones beneath my feet at times, other times grass, and occasionally, a twig or bush brushes my arm. At first, I am somewhat scared, following blind and unknowing, but at some point, the traveling gathers its own rhythm, and it inexplicably lulls me into a kind of curious calm. Even the belt of bones becomes familiar and soothing as it raps against my legs. I hold on to my memory of security in the older woman's eyes and allow myself to surrender to the odd excitement of this evening. We walk and walk and walk, and I hear nothing but the sounds of the occasional animal skulking through the brush. We walk and walk, and I still hear nothing, nothing, until I hear the distinctive crack of wood burning. Popping. And a spontaneous rush passes through my body. Without knowing why or how, I know that this is *it*. That we are approaching. My body tenses, and I stumble, losing the pace of my leader. She stops for a moment and allows me to collect myself. Then she continues.

I sense that we are in a clearing, and I can hear the roar of what sounds like several large fires. I am anxious, muscles ready to move, ready for anything. Sweat breaks out on my body. The strip of cloth binding my wrists and used to lead me is passed to another. I feel the older woman move behind me. I am tense with uncanny anticipation as she removes my blindfold, and I see you for the first time.

You stand erect, lit from behind by the fire. I recognize you right away with a rush of desire, despite everything. We are both dark-skinned, differently featured, but our eyes remain the same. I would know you anywhere. It is your hands alone I want tied to me thus. We both smile, and I feel the woman slipping away, backing into the night.

Four fires burn in ceremonial bowls on upraised wooden stands. A fifth bonfire burns massively just above the center of the circle created by the others. I am unafraid now.

You unbind my wrists and throw the cloth into the central bonfire. Its musky aroma fills the air. Your eyes never leave mine, but I break your stare to take in your body. You are ritually painted. Red and black symbols mark every inch of your surface, making you seem wild, unruly. Your hair is long and plaited at the back, although twisted strands have escaped and frame your face. Your features seem noble, your gaze intent.

Your full breasts are proudly exposed, with a giant animal claw slung on a leather string in between them. You wear a man's tribal wrap about your waist. Your gender seems to flicker and shift with the flames.

You kiss the palms of my hands and speak the first words to break the spell of silence surrounding this evening. "You asked me here to play for you."

Somehow, I know the answer. "You asked me here to dance for you."

You answer by lowering my hands and giving a kind of bow while backing away and around the bonfire to a large drum situated in front of a boulder. You sit upon the boulder and place the drum between your knees. You close your eyes. Wait.

I take my cue and turn slowly. I take in the circle, our presence, the animals covert at the edges, the energy of the fires, and plant my feet firm upon the soil. I draw up the power of the earth through my feet, feel it flow up my legs and through my trunk. I open my arms to the stars, throw back my head, and wait as well.

The throb starts slowly. I tune in to my breath, my heartbeat, the ache between my legs, the pulse of my blood in my veins, all aligning with the spinning of the planet and the tempo of the person I love, who I lust for, who sits a fire away from me, and yet whose body heat I feel like the sun upon my skin.

Your hands caress the drumskin pulled tight across the frame. You coax it, woo it like a temperamental lover. I sway, shift my weight from one foot to the other and feel the wind lift my hair. Something's growing. I open my eyes to you, and yours are already upon me. Ready.

You begin to play. A simple budding beat. The sound breaks through the night, carries in waves to my ears, and travels through my body into my feet. I step it lightly into the earth. Your hands on the skin reach me, create sensation in my own. I let the sound fill me. I allow my hips to respond as they please, moving softly in the night, my beads and bones jingling, full of small motions that become bigger. Grander. More engaged as the beat rises, becomes a pulse, a throbbing in the dark. Something insistent and seething. I feel the longing rising in my throat. My fingertips are tingling. I want more.

You stroke the drum with such focus. The beat enthralls.

Growing more intense. A thumping unrelenting and yearning. My body must move. I put my mind to enhancing the impression. Visualizing, feeling myself drawing up the molten core of the earth through my soles. Calling up the explosive inner blaze, lying unseen but riotous beneath the surface. Each strike of the drum reverberates within me; it is the uncontrollable unpredictability of passion you pound on skin, I on earth. I move with the flames, a wild thing of flashing muscle. Each action athletic, confident, sure of its significance. Can you feel me? A high-pitched ululation pierces the air. Is that you? Is it me? Are we still two separate people? I jangle my bones, glistening with the ardour of sweat. Your face is furrowed and entranced.

I dance a thank-you tribute to each corner. Thank you for this woman, this body I inhabit, this lust, this moment, my arms spell out. I appreciate your gifts. I will make much of them.

And so it is that I come to you, drawn up to my full height, proud and hungry.

You keep playing, your eyes fixed upon my body. I step up so that the drum is framed by my legs, and your hands beat between my thighs. The music pulsates, permeating me, entering me like a prophecy. It swells, grows wilder, makes me grab my breasts lustily and open my mouth to the heavens, throw back my head with my eyes to the stars, and feel the power of our animal selves. Feral, fierce.

I look down, and your wrap has fallen open. I am not surprised or upset to see you are a man. Somehow, it is tremendously erotic, more than I can bear, and I scream, rip the claw from round your neck with one hand, and push you willingly to the ground with the other. I place you impatiently inside me where the music had been and dance more, dance frantically on top of you. You lie, awesomely silent and yielding like the earth beneath you as I buck on top, bursting with violent, strange animal noises.

Red, fiery blood red, red fills my vision, burns me... and the claw is grasped too tightly in my fist, too fervent, piercing my flesh as I wail an unearthly hunger, pain a bizarre intensification of delight. We move with the whirling earth, and you keep rhythm with me, catch the fever, drive us harder and faster. Further, further into the inferno...further...hot... into the firestorm...sweltering...

❖

I woke with the feel of you warm and wet between my thighs, the scream still echoing in my mouth. I woke with an urgent need, sweat covering my body. The sheets were twisted, entrapping me. I looked over, and you were peaceful, your breathing calm and even, unaware. I could not endure it. I tore away the sheets, ripped off the blankets, and parted your thighs, still half-mad with the vision.

I awoke you with an all-consuming start. My tongue a blue-hot flame licking your body alive. I felt the tremors shake off your slumber, warm you from sleeping, arouse your senses. Mind confused, body alert, you stirred quickly to meet me as I took you. You who I'd know in any place, any fantasy, any body. The woman of my dreams.

WATER

The grass is soft under my feet, and the air is crisp, tightening my nipples under this cloth. I can barely see three feet in front of me, but I follow the sounds of your laughter as you pad your way across our backyard. I stare up at the perfect round of the moon and breathe deeply the scents of evening in our garden, earthy and sweet. When I look ahead again, I can make out your silhouette rustling in the moonlight ahead of me. You start to whoop it up and throw your nightie in the air. I pick it up, admiring your abandon. The rounds of your body heave like the tides as you run the last stretch before the pond. You glance back to me, and I can see the sparkle in your eyes. You dive into the water with a grace astounding for your years.

I don't know exactly how this began. Something about the full moon and friskiness, I suppose, but for several years now, we've been engaged with this ritual. Two old ladies bathing each other by the full summer moon. I settle on the bank and hike my cotton nightie up so it won't get wet. You come toward me, eyes flashing. I pat my thigh, and you stick out your bottom lip. I smile. You come. You nestle your head into my open lap and both of us are aware of the naked parts of our bodies, but we are moving slowly, moving around the knowledge.

I have brought the pitcher and jars. I unscrew the lid, pretending to ignore your eyes staring up at me, and I place some of the contents in my palm. I rub my hands together and run them through your hair. We are immersed in the scent of lavender. I made this shampoo from our very own garden, and this makes the odor even sweeter. Your eyes are closed now and your breathing steady. I am working my fingers along your scalp, using as much force as these old fingers contain. I am moving in circles, and I can feel your body relax into the motion. You sigh, reminding me of the newfound sensuality of these years. How we relish sensation. How much pleasure there is in something as commonplace as kneading dough. How it feels, warmed by my hands, as I make raisin bread for our grandchildren. I am awed at how tenderly I care about these enduring, soft bodies we have lived in. As if on cue, one of your tight purple nipples bobs above the surface of the water, winking at me, and it calls to me with an electric pull, reminding me of other memories.

Our first kayaking trip. Gliding through pristine lakes, watching birds soar, and hearing nothing but the steady dip of our paddles. I felt so connected to you even as we navigated the water separately. It reminded me so much of our life. I'd speed ahead to catch the first glimpse around the bend, beyond the rocks. Sometimes you'd race me—you always won, damn you—or sometimes I'd dawdle behind, absorbing something beautiful, and then you'd circle back to me. That time, it was like a dance. Like our flirtation when we first met. We took turns being cocky. We splashed one another mercilessly, showed daring, threw our heads back, and laughed long and loud.

I circled you, then took off, paddling as hard as I could, heaving all my muscle into each push of the water. You knew to follow. You passed me, shored up, then practically ripped me out of my kayak and made the fiercest love to me there on the rocks of the embankment. We were totally oblivious. It was some of the wildest sex we had. Urgent and animal. I didn't even register the heat of the sun on my flesh or the pain of the rock. I never considered the possibility of others seeing us. I don't even think we found a spot shielded from view. I loved that time, and though we fucked regularly outdoors after it, no time compared to the first because it was so spontaneous and unspoken.

Like when you began fingering me under the water at public beaches. I don't know why, but I so got off on that: your hungry fingers pulling aside my bikini bottoms, and your eyes all the while innocently looking away. Above the water line all was casual and yet all furiously searching and delving below...

Yes, we have done well with water, I think. I remember how you held me from behind in the tub as I labored to bring our first child into the world. It felt so comforting, like you were also birthing someone, like you had birthed *me* before this moment, and you had, baby, you really had. You remade me into someone unafraid to shine, and that's why I could trust your gaze when you moved out of the tub to sit beside me and hold my terrified eyes with your calm when I became afraid that I would burst from fear and pain. The clearest memory of my life is the torrent of exhilaration I felt when our first child was born into the cup of your waiting hands. Your face in that moment is etched into my body as a living memory. I laughed hysterically, and you bawled so badly that your hands were shaking with emotion, and then we always told Jailin when she was growing up that all her problems stemmed from her mother shaking her around like a rattle when she was born.

"Must've mushed up your brains. At least she didn't drop you on your head."

You always got so defensive when I told the story. "Hey now. I didn't mean to. I was scared, man!"

So I told it lots just to antagonize you. The day Jailin left for university, you were beside yourself with worry. I knew you were scared because you couldn't protect her. But we both knew we raised her right when she kissed us good-bye at the airport and then handed you a rattle and smiled with a lovely wickedness only she could compose.

Three kids meant lots of sex in the shower. The bathroom was the only place they wouldn't venture to pester us since they had somehow incontrovertibly claimed our bedroom as fair territory for unannounced interruptions. After some close calls, we quickly learned to love it up in the shower. We'd be slippery and giggling, trying not to make any noise that could be heard over the showerhead. We bought four different makes, looking for the noisiest one, laughing all the way down the hardware aisle at how pathetic our sex life had become and yet not really minding either.

We'd learned to take sex holidays. We joked about buying a boat just so that we could be alone and get laid. The first time we took off on the boat, though, we were so aching for each other that we spent the entire week making love below deck and then had a hell of a time explaining our lack of a tan to everyone. After that, we used the first day of the trip to tan. I turned it into a perverse form of torture by purchasing a new bikini every time and by placing myself in provocative positions on deck as much as possible. Then, no matter how much you begged me, I would refuse to go below deck with you until the first nightfall.

"Thank God," you'd growl, pulling me down the stairs, body tensed with anticipation once we had watched the sun set on the water together. It was magic to lie in your arms, rocked by the waves and bathing in the vibrant colors of the sun as it dipped beneath the shimmer of the water. I could feel your heart beating beneath my head as I snuggled into you. I could feel your breath on my forehead. I'd close my eyes and feel the rhythms of your breathing, your heart, and the waves and wonder at the rhythm you'd choose to move my hips to soon...very soon.

When we were young, before the children, the sex was more energetic but somehow not as intimate as it became once our lives were more entangled. You were a visitor to my flesh, then, and I expected a drama to be played upon me as an entrance fee. I was not sure about you, but then one day, you delivered. We were hanging out at my apartment, stripped down to T-shirts and underwear in the muggy August heat. I was lying sideways on my futon, arms dangling over the edges, feet pressed high on the wall. I was whining about the heat, boredom, the fact that my parents wouldn't spring for a "goddamned air-conditioner."

You straddled me, your full weight bearing down on me. "Don't you ever stop complaining?"

I was shocked beyond words. Before I could feel insulted, you whipped off your T-shirt, exposing your full breasts just inches from my mouth, and I was confused. Your intentions became much clearer once you had me spread-eagled in the door frame of my bedroom and teased my writhing body with an ice cube between your teeth.

Those were good times, and I am purring in the back of my throat as I remember, massaging your neck and scalp. How long have we been sitting here? I lose myself so often now, and yet I have never felt so present. There is so much silence between us now. It amuses me. So many years of talking your ear off and now so quiet. Oh well, we don't need to use our lips that way anymore. Such a waste of precious energy when there are so many more lovely ways to use them. To be over sixty and constantly horny is a surprising and sweet thing. Of course, between the arthritis in your fingers and my back pain, we are not so act-driven as we once were, but all of our motions now are somehow infused with a tender desire for the other.

I stop massaging and bend to fill the pitcher with pond water. This pitcher we brought back from a trek to Turkey, where we smelled the true smell of wild roses and danced in circles of women on sacred sites. I think about the story of everything in our home every time I see or use them now, and so when I rinse your hair with this pitcher, I can almost taste the sweetness of the fresh chickpeas we ate under a bower of wildflowers, the breeze blowing my scarf so that it almost caressed your face as you sat across from me.

"Darling."

I am back in the pond, and you are standing in front of me, torso above water, flesh dripping.

"Yes?"

"I want to get you *wet*." Your eyes are dancing, feisty, and I know that I've been warned. I know what you are about to do, and I permit it. You wrap your arms around my waist and whirl me into the water with you. You know I prefer to take my time, unlike you, who craves the cold slap of the water overwhelming you. I know that you probably saw me drifting off into my own reveries and wanted to bring me back, thrill me with an unusual sensation, shake things up, and I appreciate your intentions. I laugh warmly so you know.

My nightie has a strange weight to it, and it clings to me. "This feels nice," I murmur, motioning down to the fabric plastered across my chest and floating around my knees.

"Does it?" You swim closer and try to swim under the skirt, but I splash away. Suddenly you are over me, my back is pressed against the bank, and your eyes are flashing with fire. You are holding me again. With your eyes and your arms like so many times before. If I close my eyes right now, I could fall into an endless succession of such holdings, but I don't close my eyes because I want to be in this one. Your hands are searching, and I acquiesce, but the water is too wet, and I am too old. It steals my moisture from you, and so you smoothly shift gears.

"Let's get you out of here and out of these wet clothes." We help each other out of the pond, and you try to help me out of the nightie, but it gets stuck around my head. You begin to laugh, and I get scared, stuck in a mess of wet cloth. I can feel you shaking and curse you, realizing how ridiculous I must look: a droopy old lady standing half-naked in her backyard with wet pajamas stuck around her head. I can't see you because my face is covered and because you're on the ground, holding your belly with tears streaming out of your eyes.

"Goddamnit! Stop laughing and help me." I'm trying to stay mad, but it's contagious, and I laugh too, and then between laughing and struggling I fall over, and my ass is hanging out, and my arms are over my head, and I'm thinking, "I don't think I've ever laughed so hard," and you're tugging and laughing, tugging and laughing, until finally, it pops off. I can see you're still hysterical, and I look around, despite myself, knowing that no one can see us.

"You're a shithead," I muster, clambering up with as much dignity as possible. You still can't talk, your face all mushed up, waving my nightgown around in explanation, so I grab it roughly from you and stalk off in mock disgust, though I'm careful to let you see a hint of a smile. And then you are padding up behind me. You try to grab me, but I whip around and snap at you with the wet nightie.

"Leave me alone, you!" But you grab for me again, and we both fall down, great bubbles of laughter bursting out despite myself, and we sit awhile in the warm belly feeling of it until the silence we know so well sets back in.

"One of us could have broken a hip, you know," I say. There is a pause and another bright round of laughter.

"Let me see those hips," you say with a growl, the flame distinct in your voice. And so, my eyes on the fullness of the moon and my body supported by the earth, once again, I open to you.

PART SIX: NOW AND FOREVER
LONG-TERM LOVE EROTICA

Good Clean Fun

I like to make Ella wait. I like her naked and wanting, watching as I lay out the instruments of her pleasure. One by one by one. Each movement precise. Intentional. My hand lingering to arrange each item just so. A still art arrangement of promised pleasure. I take my time, hum and sway to the music giving rhythm and tone to our time together. I ignore her. Though she makes it hard. Any time her tits are out, it's hard. Hard to focus. Hard to stay away. But I do. For a time. I lay out the implements. I breathe and gather my power to lead this scene between us. I breathe and face her.

She's lying on our bed, propped up on her elbow, watching me expectantly. The drop sheet is already beneath her. I light the first candle and tell her to turn onto her stomach. She takes her long blond hair and ties it up in a quick, untidy bun high on top of her head before obeying. She knows where we are going. I mean, we've been together a long time now. Before I met Ella, I used to worry about sex becoming boring in a long-term, monogamous relationship. But instead, I found the structure and familiarity surprisingly comforting and liberating. There is nothing stale in the playful predictability between us. What is known deepens. What isn't yet known is sought. All with this incredibly strong and dependable connection I didn't know existed before her.

She settles down happily on the bed, wiggling her butt

cutely with anticipation. I pour a small amount of mineral oil onto my hands and begin to lightly massage her shoulders, working my way down to her lower back. I remove my hands and note her relaxed smile and the thin sheen of the oil covering her. Now we make art.

I wipe my hands clean and eye my choices. Where to begin? Green is my favorite color, so let's start there. I select the green candle, hold its wick to the flame of the first candle, and watch it catch fire. I stand over my gorgeous girlfriend and begin nice and easy, holding the candle high, allowing one tiny drip at a time to dot her exposed back. She's breathing deeply, relaxed and comfortable. I move the green candle to my left hand and pick up the blue one with my right, alighting it and adding new drops of color to my canvas. I start varying the height of the candles, and her breathing shifts, as does the intensity of the heat shocking her pale, smooth skin. I enjoy watching how her anticipation becomes tinged with apprehension, and I imagine her wondering where it will fall and how it will feel.

This goes on for quite some time. Until I think "enough with pointillism" and place the two candles down on the tray by the side of the bed so I can light a third that is plum-colored. I hold it mid-height over her torso and just…consider. Ella is holding her breath. I can tell. It makes me smile, and I splash wax between her shoulder blades. Her body jumps, and she makes a small sound of surprise. I laugh and grab the blue candle.

"Now don't move and wreck my art," I warn her as I begin pouring horizontal lines of wax across the middle of her back. I let the wax slip down her sides, knowing this feels maddening. I move slowly, predictably, create a pattern of expectation for her with my carefully spaced lines. She's relaxing into the pattern, and so am I. It's lulling and pleasant. Maybe too pleasant. I can't have too much of that, so I stop. I stand back and consider the colors, shapes and sensations so far. Time for some red, I think.

I light the red candle and hold it in my left hand. I prep several to be used in my right. Ella waits. Her eyes are closed, and she is humming quietly, un-self-consciously to the music. She's so fucking adorable; it's ridiculous. I remind her not move and set myself up over top of her. I like this moment, so I draw it out. Stand there with melting wax flaming in my upraised hands, as a beautiful, loving woman waits expectantly below me. Then I let the red wax spill in a steady stream from on high, moving it in a spiral, moving it ever closer, allowing it to pool in the small of her lower back. She begins to squirm slightly, and I watch carefully now, knowing the pooling becomes intense, looking to dance precisely on the edge between pleasure and pain. I splash, drop, drip, and apply random amounts of other colors on her shoulder blades and upper back while still pooling and swirling the red wax on her lower back.

"You good?" I whisper as I see tension rising in her body.

She doesn't answer besides a "Mmm" and I see her toes are clenched, and she's sweaty, so I stop with the red candle and focus on her upper back, easing up on the heat factor and focusing more on finishing my masterpiece. Her body looks incredible. I mean, I have Jackson Pollocked the shit out of her back. It's impressive. I create a few more shapes and add a final splash of color to a surprisingly blank spot under her left shoulder blade.

She jumps, and I laugh and say, "Stay still…it will crack."

But she tells me to "Piss off," and then we're both laughing for no really good reason except that we're happy. The wax is mostly cooled now, except the most recent additions, so it really is beginning to crack and flake.

"Stay put," I say as I blow out the candles and go to grab my camera. We have a whole private album of wax art. It's kind of our thing. I've done some pretty cool stuff with it, if I do say so myself. Her favorite was a giant mandala. Intricate, pretty, and challenging to create with precision. My favorite was when I wrote a super dirty poem up her legs and back. Now that was hard. Once I made a birthday cake on her belly with her tits as two of the candles. It wasn't *my* birthday, but I made a dirty wish all the same and blew out those candles real good.

Most nights, though, it's just random, abstract, whatever art like tonight. I play with the lighting and the angles, trying to capture her sexiness just right. And damn, she is sexy. So sexy. I put down the camera and start to climb onto the bed with her. She goes to turn over to see what I'm up to, but I push her back down.

"You don't listen very well. Keep still." I lie beside her, and she turns her head to the other side so we can kiss. Sweetly. So sweetly. I can never get enough of the taste of her little lips on mine. I brush my hand lightly over the tiny mounds of wax on her back until I reach her ass, round and soft and desperately in need of a good squeezing. I kindly oblige and knead her ass for a time, still kissing her gently. My fingers move lower. Seeking her out. She wiggles assistance, willing my fingers to find what they seek. And she is wet and already ready. We break our kiss to smile at one another.

"Are you going to listen?" I ask.

"Do I ever?"

We both smirk, and I get up to move to a better position on my knees, closer to her ass. I start kneading her vulva with my fist, letting my knuckles create a strong rhythmic force for her clit. She's already moaning and moving her hips. Wax is breaking off all over the bed. I stop what I'm doing to smack her ass. Hard.

"I said don't move," I remind her. I smack her again, pleased to see her ass is already pinking up. "I worked hard on that wax art. Don't fucking wreck it." I can see from here that she's smirking, and I throw a few more slaps in for good cautionary measure before returning to her pussy.

And by returning, I mean slipping two fingers inside, knowing she likes to be surprised and that she's ready. She gasps and starts writhing against me. I finger-fuck her well, just the way I know she likes it, till she's bucking up against me and thrashing around so blatantly that I really have no choice but to continue punishing her. Punishing and pleasing, pleasing and punishing until finally, she comes in the sweet familiar way I love, and we crash down together on the bed, spent and smiling.

"You're a mess," I say, noting the pieces of cold broken wax mixed with her hair. The thing is, though, I love pretty girls in disarray. Ella is tiny, baby-doll, feminine, gorgeous, like the girl my mom always wanted me to be: pretty, perky, china doll, girlie, perfect. Like when we get dressed up for a night out, her hair, her makeup, her outfit, everything is on point. Plus, she's a clean freak perfectionist most of the time, so dirtying her up is definitely my all-time favorite pastime. I don't know why, but a slightly disheveled attractive woman turns me on.

In university, we studied this poem called "Delight in Disorder" by Robert Herrick, and I was blown away by the recognition that someone else living more than four hundred years ago had the same turn-on as me. That he too felt there was nothing sexier than a lady in a state of slight disorder. I remember the lines even today, though I amuse myself by updating the words:

A sweet disorder in the dress
Kindles in me a wantonness.
A messy bun fixed up in haste
Makes me desire a little taste.
An erring bra strap here and there
Enthralls the frisky dyke in there.

A zipper neglectful and thereby
I start to wonder if she's not shy.
A winning ass, deserving note
Makes my breath catch in my throat.
A careless G-string, in whose peek
I see the place for which I seek.
These more bewitch me than when art
Is too precise in every part.

"Let's get you cleaned up," I say, knowing she's dying to shower. But first we need to remove the wax. This might just be my favorite part, as she lies still, fully trusting beneath my confident hands, as I carefully scrape wax from her flesh with a blade. A safe knife, one designed for wax play, but no less oddly psychologically thrilling to trace along her contours. For it resonates with danger even as we both know it's safe. Plus, the sensation of wax removal is just one of those oddly satisfying tactile impressions like…like scooping out a ripe avocado or fitting something slightly smaller just perfectly into something bigger. It's inexplicably gratifying on a purely sensational level.

We make it to the shower…eventually. Our favorite place. The one thing we splurged on in this new house of ours. Because Ella is obsessed with shower sex. Which is ironic and fits, given my own fetish with dirtying girls up. She's eager to please me back, and the second we're in, she's on me, but I tell her she's benched because she didn't listen. She laughs and tries to touch me, but I grab her hands and hold them.

"I'm serious. You just get to watch." I see indecision flit across her eyes, but she settles on playing along and takes a spot on the bench, passively defiant with arms crossed. Oh, did I mention that our shower is so huge it has a freaking bench in it? Yeah. See. Splurge. It also has the world's best showerhead. Like better than any vibrator you ever owned, practically infinite settings, must have been designed by a woman, so thank God for female engineers, world's best showerhead.

I set to work, cleaning my body in the most luxuriously sensual manner I can manage, making sure she has a good view of all her favorite parts as I soap them. I smirk her way the entire time, soaping myself up really good and clean for her viewing pleasure. She squirms on the bench, seething frustration my way, but she stays put. I detach the showerhead and begin to touch myself, trying to forget she's watching because I still feel strange having her see me do this, although she begs me to do it all the time because she likes to watch. I alternate between my hands and the showerhead until my legs are starting to shake, and I need to decide how I want to end this. I look over at Ella, and she's resentful and hungry but determined all at once, and frankly, it amuses me, so I linger a bit more on the edge of orgasm.

But then I worry that I might slip over without her, and so I bark instructions at her. She moves eagerly from the bench, allowing me to take her place. She knows how I like to finish and kneels enthusiastically before me as I settle into position, one leg up on the bench, giving her just enough room to place her mouth on me. I run the hot water up and down, and up and down her back as she pleases me like only she can, this girl I love so much, so fucking much I can't even handle it. And between her skillful mouth and the thought of being lucky enough to love like this, I come loud and powerful in the shower of the home we share. Just another Tuesday night for this boring, long-term, monogamous couple. Just another Tuesday night full of good clean fun.

HOW I REALLY MET MY WIFE

We all had different reasons for being in that room. There were the ready, polished excuses we offered to others and then murkier motivations too. We believed our excuses with varying degrees of naïveté and denial. But whatever brought us there, there we were: Jake, naked on the futon, clearly excited, Monique, trembling visibly in attractive uncertainty, and me, Alex, jaded at only twenty-five, leading the show in my lingerie.

Those were not our real names. But then nothing that happened in that room was ever real for me. Until she came along.

My wife and I can never tell people the truth of how we met, so we lie. We agreed long ago on an acceptably cute and romantic tale that would fit with the mainstream, middle-class, suburban life that we live. Because everyone knows that happy families don't begin in erotic massage parlors.

Except that ours did.

The best lies contain a kernel of pure truth, so here are the lies that we told about why we were there. I was a university student, the first in my family to attend, and I was finishing up a very expensive degree. She was a newly single young mother, looking to make money to fight for sole custody of her daughter. He was an arrogant prick cheating on his wife. Okay, so that's not fair, but neither was what he was doing. Though I was hardly in a position to judge…not that it stopped me.

Jake was one of my regulars. I didn't have a lot of them because I refused to string men along with flirty suggestions that maybe more might happen between us in time if we got close enough. I wasn't into having a work boyfriend who would buy me gifts and ask me about my real life. This was all business for me, and I was totally upfront and in charge. That was part of the appeal: that I could boss men around and feel like I was taking advantage of them for once. Jake stuck with me, though, because he was, as mentioned previously, an arrogant prick. He was young to be frequenting a massage parlor, and he was ridiculously hot, and he knew it. He walked into the place like he expected all of us to catfight and claw each other's eyes out over the chance to touch his naked flesh. I suspect he picked me precisely because I seemed supremely uninterested.

Men don't expect to find lesbians working in a rub-and-tug. But men don't gross me out. They just don't turn me on. I know plenty of my Sapphic sisters would balk at the idea of giving a guy the standard "happy ending" hand-job to finish off an erotic massage, but it was never a big deal for me. I'd run my hands along their body, wriggling in my lingerie in what I judged to be an appealingly sensual manner. They'd feel up my tits and beg to feel more. I'd refuse in a firm but flirty way. If they were regulars and I knew that they would respect my boundaries, I'd give them a good view of my pussy, straddling their face and keeping it just out of reach. If they were new, I'd simply lie with them, continuing the whole sensual wriggling thing before the standard ending: the jacking of their cock. They'd come, and I'd make a bunch of money. That was how it worked. That was the routine. It was almost robotic for me after the first month. Honestly, in my mind, I was usually reviewing things I needed to remember for the next exam. I was never wet. I was never tempted to do more. At least not with the clients. But with my coworkers… well, that was another story.

The moment Jenny stepped through the door of Taboo, my heart inexplicably clenched. She looked so lost and out of place and yet was putting on a fiercely brave front that was only betrayed by the wild gleam of her eyes and the way every action she took was jerky, as if she was holding back and then pushing herself to overcome the resistance. Every girl in the place was giving her an immediate, calculated once-over. How pretty was she? How threatening? Which clients would go to her now? Would she get along or be a bitch? She was a petite little blond thing with dark, keen brown eyes. She struck me right away as a small and perhaps adrift but formidably determined woman. I wanted to know her and her story from the very beginning. Luckily, my manager was a lazy party girl who managed nothing much more than snorting coke and passing off her minor work responsibilities to me. She decided that I should train Jenny the next day.

Jenny decided to go by Monique, which seemed all wrong to me. I didn't think she could pull the name off. Monique sounded sophisticated and street-smart, whereas this girl, for all her feisty resolve, seemed pretty naïve. But maybe our work names were all aspirational. I picked Alex because it was gender-neutral enough to sound strong. I didn't want clients thinking they could get away with anything, and the name was a kind of warning that I would not be a touchy-feely, giggly, silly girl.

We opened around noon, and I walked "Monique" through the routines. She listened attentively and nodded. If she was panicking, she managed to hide it. I'm not sure I hid my desire as well as she hid her fear. Monique wore a cute schoolgirl kilt with a rather transparent white blouse that showed off the black bra beneath it. I'd seen my coworkers try to pull off the sexy schoolgirl look before but never this successfully. Jenny embodied the unnerving, paradoxical mixture of coquettish innocence and sultry cunning that whispered Lolita for anyone attuned to that particular kink. Maybe that was what drew me to her too. The enigma of her contradictory vulnerability and strength.

It was pretty dead that afternoon, so we were able to talk for a long time. Most of the other girls spent any dead time watching the little TV in the waiting area, but I usually spent my time studying. That day, I studied Jenny. I was a pretty good student, but damn, if I had studied for my classes the way I studied her face and words, I would have earned enough scholarship money to quit this stupid job. Her skirt was ridiculously short. Its pleats swayed in time with her bottom every time she got up to go anywhere, and I caught the briefest glimpse of ass cleavage once or twice. How could I not be bewitched? My fingers ached to inch up her thighs beneath that little red kilt and discover the secrets it hid. Of course, my mind filled up with ludicrous, clichéd fantasies of taking her over my knee and punishing her for her too-short skirt. Making her stand at attention and measuring her hemline to her finger lengths drawn out along her pale, quivering thigh. It was hard to concentrate on reality when her outfit inspired such easy fantasy.

She offered her rehearsed excuse right away. "I'm not going to be here for long," she began. "I'm just trying to make some money to fight my ex for sole custody."

"You're a mom?" I asked, surprised given her age and diminutive stature.

She bristled. "I'm just doing what I've got to do. All I want to do is take my daughter and run away, but I'm stuck in this shithole city until I can prove he doesn't deserve custody."

"I'm not judging. Trust me, no one thinks they'll wind up here, and no one plans to stay. It's no big deal that you're a mom. A couple of the girls here have kids."

"Yeah, well, like I said, it's just temporary. Until I can save enough for the lawyer."

"Sure."

I learned that Jenny can't stand silence. She'll fill it with any kind of inane blather. Perhaps that was why she started sharing about her ex. I certainly wasn't prying enough to ask. Her eyes teared up at one point when she talked about the moment she'd stopped making excuses and realized her boyfriend was abusive. She excused herself to go to the bathroom then, but we both knew she was really going there to cry in privacy. Before the first client arrived, Jenny had pretty much shared her entire life story, told in a defensive rush. She clearly wasn't at ease with her decision to work here. and I found myself wanting to protect her and make her way easier.

I found myself wanting to do other things too. Sometimes while she talked, her words just fell away, and I was left mesmerized, watching the shapes made by her mouth. She had nice teeth. Her lips were a little thin, but I liked the planes of her face. Her eyes were so dark brown that they were almost black. They were also sharp and missed nothing.

"Why are you staring at me?"

"Am I? Sorry. I was just listening."

"No, you weren't. You were staring."

This kind of blunt, direct challenge would be a difficult characteristic of her interactions with me for years. She is the brusque truth-teller in the relationship, and I am the tactful diplomat. Both roles have their place, I know, but I really wish she'd learn to soften her edges a bit.

At that time, Jake was always coming to see me directly after work on Fridays. He said it started off his weekend right. He strolled through the door at his usual time, ego and privilege radiating from him as he filled the room at once with his booming voice and macho energy.

"Where's my girl at? Jake needs to start his weekend off right."

I motioned for Jenny to follow me and went to greet Jake,

rolling my eyes internally at his annoying habit of speaking of himself in the third person.

"Whoa! Who's this new cutie?" Jake bellowed. I watched him turn on the charm even thicker and grab her hand to place a kiss. "Milady," he said, as though he were a knight and she a damsel in distress.

"This is Jake. Don't let him fool you. He's a dick."

"Alex, I'm shocked and hurt. After all this time, I still haven't convinced you of what a great guy I am? You know, I never have to work this hard with anyone else." He winked and made to manhandle me right there in the lobby, but I evaded him by moving behind the front desk to write down the details of his visit.

"I assume you're looking for the usual today, Jake. Would it be okay if Monique here tags along? I'm training her. There'd be no extra cost to you."

"Two for the price of one, eh? I'd say this is gonna be an amazing weekend," Jake said, looking Monique up and down lasciviously.

"Great. You know the drill. Go get undressed and relax and wait for us. We'll be there in a few minutes."

"Okay, but don't take too long, cutie." Jake placed his man paws on Monique's ass and pulled her in close. "I'm excited to see what you've got going on under this little skirt of yours."

"Okay, okay, Jake. Go easy on the new girl, please. Don't scare her off. Get inside," I said, shooing him away.

He sauntered off, whistling to himself, and I turned to Jenny to assess how she was doing. She had a concerned look on her face, and I began to worry that she might back out. "What's wrong?" I asked.

"He's wearing a wedding ring."

"Yeah. He's a dick. I told you." This didn't seem to reassure her, so I kept talking. "Look, that's the deal. Most of them are married, but they've got a million excuses. Their marriage is a sham, and they're only staying together for the kids. It's not really cheating because it's not sex. She has no time for him now with the new baby. She got fat. Whatever. I feel badly about their wives, I do, but I'm not the one betraying them. I'm just trying to better my life. And some of the guys are sweet."

She looked dubious, so I rushed on. "Seriously. One of my regulars is an amputee who lost his arm in a freak work accident. His girlfriend left him right after it. And you can imagine that it's not exactly easy to date when you're partially dismembered, so he comes here for some human touch and connection. I totally get and respect that. And I really like him. A lot of guys are just lonely and want to be touched. It's a lot easier for women to get touch whenever we want it, right? Honestly, sometimes they pay me just to hold them and talk. It's sad actually. But then there are the married jerks, like Jake. It's a mixed bag. But that's the job. Think you can you handle it?"

She took a deep breath and seemed to gather herself in tightly. "Yes, let's do this." We went back to the waiting area and began to change into our lingerie. It was all I could do to keep my eyes focused on the floor. I didn't want to freak her out, but I was dying to see what she would wear.

"Is this okay?" she asked, adjusting her boobs in a tight-fitting purple lace negligee. My heart rate sped up, and I swallowed self-consciously before nodding, not trusting my voice as my eyes wandered approvingly up and down her compact curves. I took a breath and gathered myself too. I had to get it together and lead this interaction, I reminded myself.

"Okay," I began. "Jake always pays for an hour-long reverse. That means we have to stretch things out at least forty-five minutes, or he'll complain. The reverse means he gets to 'massage' us too, which is really just code for he can touch us, but where he touches is completely up to you. Some girls allow them to touch between their legs and some don't. Whatever you decide, you've got to be clear and consistent across the clients, as some of them talk."

"I'd rather not, but will it matter for making money?" she asked bluntly.

"Yes and no. Obviously, the girls who allow it get more clients, but they tend to be nasty cheapskates, and I don't want them anyway. I'd rather do less work for more pay, you know? Plus, you don't know where their hands have been. Or you do, actually. Jake's totally playing with himself right now, waiting for us. I'd rather keep it clean, and I always just tell them that if I let all the guys touch me there, they wouldn't want to. Most of them don't like being reminded that they share us with others. And they don't want to think about how that could get pretty dirty, you know? On the other hand, some guys revel in that thought, to be honest, but again, they're not the guys I want."

"Okay, got it."

I hesitated before plunging on. "All right. The other thing is that, usually with a double, there's a little show the girls put on for the guys. Just kind of making out with each other to get them going. Each girl is different in how far she takes it. Again, it's totally up to you," I said, literally holding my breath waiting to see how she would respond.

She pondered a moment, then burst out laughing. "I've never kissed a girl before. That will be weird but maybe kind of fun." I would remind her of this line many times in our weird but fun future together. In that moment, however, I just felt relief and desire flood through me. I led the way into the massage room with an unusual thrill of actual erotic energy coursing through me.

Indeed, Jake was already hard and stroking away as we came into the room and prepared to touch him. Jake had turned on the gas fireplace and selected the music. He jumped up, and his dick bounced around as he made way for us on the bed.

"Ladies first," he said, motioning mock-gallantly to the bed. "I don't think I've ever had a double with you, Alex. Let's see what kind of show you put on."

I made my way to the bed and beckoned to Monique to join me. She did so, trembling visibly. I tried to forget that Jake was there and just took Monique's face in my hands and caressed her hair. Her eyes were wide and shining with a combination of fear, curiosity, resolve, and perhaps a hint of lust. I kissed her cheek and whispered in her ear, too quietly for Jake to hear, "Just say 'I'm good' when you want to stop, okay?"

She nodded slightly, and Jake boomed too loudly, "Touch her tits, Alex. I wanna see her titties." I felt her stiffen in my arms and turned to give Jake the stink-eye.

"Jake, you're a fucking buffoon. Lean against the wall, watch, and don't say anything. I mean it."

"Why are you always so angry and mean, Alex? I kind of like it. But you kind of scare me." He laughed nervously.

"Good. I'll get scarier if you don't start listening. Monique is new, and this is her first massage. If you don't want to scare her off so that you never get the chance to see her titties, then just stay over there, jerk off, and shut up the fuck up until I tell you otherwise."

Jake was used to having women fawn over him and throw themselves at him. The fact that I bossed him around and belittled him both confused and excited him. He did as he was told. And I could admit that, from another woman's perspective, he would have made a gorgeous sight: a beautiful blond Adonis of a man, muscled and tanned, pumping away at his straining cock, desiring us, and holding back with great effort. In truth, I liked torturing him as much as he liked being tortured. Our connection was always kind of twisted.

It was the strangest thing in my life that my connection with my wife started there, in this moment, on the futon between a roaring fake fire and a horny man in a phony spectacle of lesbian desire that somehow morphed into real intimacy. It was so freaking quintessentially queer.

I looked her in the eyes, smiled, and brought my lips to hers. The kiss was tentative and gentle at first, but it didn't take long to spark to a hungry exploration of each other's mouths and bodies. Her hands wandered on my silky black negligee, and I relaxed out of my worries about freaking her out. She was responding eagerly, and at times, I wasn't even sure that I was the one leading the show anymore. She was a little firecracker of energy. I let one strap of my negligee fall and shrugged a little until one of my breasts became exposed.

Jake yelled, "Now we're talking," and I immediately tucked my tit away.

"I believe I was very clear about your role in this interaction, Jake. What part of 'shut the fuck up and jerk off' was too complex for your dumb jock brain to understand?" He mimed zipping his lip and played with his balls a bit, watching lecherously.

"You *are* really mean to him." Monique laughed.

"That's how he likes me," I replied. "Don't worry. I'm not like that to everyone. And you'll find your own dynamic with each client. In time, you'll find your way. Now, where were we?" I asked coyly, slipping a finger under one of her negligee straps, a question clear in my eyes. She blushed, and nodded, and I freed her boobs from their constraint. They were small, like her frame, but softer and more elastic than I expected until I remembered that she had a kid. It was an uncomfortable thought, and I pushed it away.

"You like what you see, Jake?" I purred, changing my position to jiggle her tits from behind. I put her on display and watched as Jake squirmed. I squeezed and caressed her breasts, playing with her nipples, kissing her neck and nibbling on her ear. She began to moan and so did Jake. My heart was beating wildly, and my pussy was drenched. I'd never been this turned on, even during other doubles. The other girls at Taboo mostly just endured it the way I did with clients. It was a completely bogus girl-on-girl simulation. They tossed their hair, trailed their long nails, made some noise, and just copied what they'd seen in porn. A little light fondling with inviting eye contact and the guy was done for. A fast track to quick money. But this was different. When this girl made searing eye contact, it was with me, not him.

"Jake's a dirty boy, Monique. I bet he wants to see your sweet little pussy. Should we let him see?"

She surprised me then. I didn't yet know that when Jenny commits to something, she goes all in. She stood and wiggled out of her lingerie, eyes blazing. Then she strode over to Jake, wearing only a tiny little matching G-string. I watched hungrily as her ass jiggled away from me. Jealousy surged through me as she gave her attention to him. I struggled to remember myself and the truth of the situation as she explored his body with her hands, and he felt up her tits. He looked at me and wisely said nothing, a smirk playing around the corners of his mouth.

"You want to see my sweet little pussy, Jake? You want to touch me?" Monique teased.

He looked at me, and I nodded, so he blurted, "Hell yeah!" She was pressing her body into his and undulating there in time to the music as his cock nestled in tightly to her torso, brushing against her breasts.

She grabbed his nipples then, and twisted hard. "Well, I don't let assholes touch me." Jake squirmed under her touch as if surprised. "You can't even be bothered to take off your damn wedding ring before you grab my tits? What the fuck is wrong with you?"

Jake looked at me accusingly, but I just laughed. I had no idea she'd play along and up the ante in our tormented dynamic. I found it hilarious and super hot. She was so tiny, and he was so huge. It was funny to watch her put him in his place. "I'll let you see my pussy, Jake. You can watch while

Alex touches it. You can even come close. But don't you dare touch me. You just touch yourself. And if you're a really good boy, I'll let you come on my tits. Understand?"

Jake nodded mutely and enthusiastically.

She strode back to me then, and I believe it was fair to say that I was enamored from that moment forward. I thought she was lost and needed protection? This chick was a force to be reckoned with. How did she ever let some man abuse her? It felt inconceivable. But then I realized that maybe she was working out something about her relationships with men through this job. Just like me, a small voice in my head admitted.

She returned to my side on the bed and kissed me feverishly. Jake crouched by the edge of the futon like some weird outsider.

"Please fuck me," she said frankly.

I'd never actually had sex with any of the girls at Taboo. It was all a silly show, and I'd only been with two other women before, so her words both thrilled and terrified me. But I looked down at her beautiful body and something inside me stirred deeply. I wanted to love her more than I'd wanted anything in a long time. I brought my mouth to her curves and lavished attention on them. I kissed, licked, bit, fondled, caressed and squeezed every piece of her that I could before hesitating at the soft strip of fuzz between her thighs.

"Are you sure?" I asked.

"Show me what I've been missing," she challenged, eyebrow cocked. And I must have done so because we've been together ever since.

We worked at Taboo for another year and made a killing with our doubles, shamelessly exploiting our sexual connection for shitloads of money. Jenny won custody, and I graduated. We quit the industry and moved in together. I had an insta-family, and all in all, through the usual ups and downs, we've made a good life together.

Our beginning is not the fairy-tale story most people are

used to hearing, so we don't tell it. We tell an innocuous lie and feel a thrill of transgression run through us with each telling. Holding hands at Little League practice, talking to the other moms. We remember Jake, poor fool. We remember Monique and Alex and the way that they brought us together. A strange, edgy backstory to our current white picket-fence reality. I look around at the other moms and wonder. *Whose husband is feeling up the latest version of Alex and Monique? Who else has secrets as juicy as us? What is real in the façade that we present to each other?*

But then I look over at my wife, cheering fiercely for our daughter clumsily rounding the bases, and I remember that the best love stories involve beating the odds. Well, in our story, there was all kinds of odd and plenty of different kinds of beating. Even now, as I recall our story and watch her clapping for our kid with proud mama-bear enthusiasm, my heart inexplicably clenches, skipping a beat. Just like the first time I saw her. And the heart never lies.

MAKE BELIEVE

My favorite part of sex is the anticipation. The build-up. I like a good backstory and some mental stimulation before our bodies get going. Perhaps that's why I took so long to find a partner. That and the fact that dating pretty much requires socializing with strangers, whether online or in person, something I have never been good at. My childhood report cards all contained some variation of the line "Alyssa is encouraged to come out of her shell more often and participate in class."

But I never understood this criticism. I was deeply engaged in my schooling. I spent a lot of time thinking about the things I was learning and extending the ideas into my own areas of interest. But because I rarely raised my hand to speak, I was not participating? And why do extroverts never understand that some of us like to live in our proverbial shells, thank you very much? My shell is comfy and quiet and just right for me.

What outgoing people don't seem to understand is that even though I was alone a lot before I met Mel, I was never lonely. My mind has always been such a rich playground of thoughts and fantasies that I could amuse myself quite happily for vast stretches of time, with just a few close friends and family members to balance out my natural inclination to solitude. My brother jokingly started to call me "the spinster" when I hit my thirtieth birthday without seeming to have dated anyone. And he was right. I hadn't. Not in any meaningful way.

When COVID-19 hit in 2020 and the series of lockdowns started, I scoffed at the extroverts freaking out and just hunkered down to lose myself in videogames, a favorite pastime that has always inspired a lot of personal fanfiction and crafting projects. I managed better than most, but even so, once COVID became a nightmare of the past, I found myself oddly longing to be around people, and so I bought a ticket to the Niagara Falls Comic-Con Convention, hoping to geek out with others who shared similar interests.

It was not a well-thought-out plan. Crowds have always been a struggle for me. And I hadn't been around large groups of people in well over a year. It was strange to see so many maskless faces. I felt bombarded and overwhelmed with stimulation. At one point, I started to have a panic attack. My heart racing and my palms sweating, I stumbled toward the outer wall of the hall, bumping into people and vendors all along the way. I spotted a window and made for it, figuring the view of the greenery outside would calm me. Unfortunately, it only showed a metallic sea of cars in a parking lot, but I leaned my head against the cool of the glass nonetheless and tried to slow my breathing.

That was when Mel rescued me. Or that's how I like to think of it anyway. It was nothing really. Just a nice person checking up on a stranger who looked as though they were upset. But it's my love story, and if I want to exaggerate and say that she showed up like a knight in shining armor to rescue the damsel in distress, then that's my prerogative.

"Are you okay? Do you need help?"

The first words my future wife said to me. I raised my eyes to her and somehow magically knew that I wouldn't be an old maid after all. I mean, it had to be fate; we were dressed in complementary costumes, both of us female warriors from our favorite videogame but in differing installments, she a Spartan mercenary and me a Viking berserker.

For no apparent reason, I started laughing. I don't know why she had that effect on me. Maybe I was just overwhelmed. Whatever the reason, she took it as a sign of hysteria, I'm sure, and she suggested that maybe some fresh air would do me good and offered to accompany me outside. The rest, as they say, is herstory.

And now we return here each year to celebrate our anniversary at this quirky gathering of nerdy misfits and superfans. All year long, we plan our characters and outfits. This year's get-up is a doozy: Queen Marie Antoinette and her rumored lesbian lover, la Princesse de Lamballe. We keep upping the ante, and I went full out this year, doing a ton of research to get the smallest details right. I've worn plenty of corsets in my cosplay time, so I'm used to the way it impedes my breathing and movement, but the pannier is really pushing the limits of my patience. This undergarment makes me three times as wide as usual out the sides, but unlike a crinoline, it is oddly flat at the front and back so that the rich embroidery at the front of the dress can be better displayed. Perhaps ideal for a spacious and ornate eighteenth-century ballroom but hardly easy to wear as one maneuvers about in a packed convention hall looking for one's wife.

We always arrive separately. Take two rooms. Re-meet, if you will. A sexy little tradition where we re-enact our first encounter. Those are the rules. Whatever our two characters in any particular year, Mel has to approach me and say as her opener, "Are you okay? Do you need help?" I don't know why, but it turns us both on to keep replaying that moment in different guises. I guess it's that those words were the beginning of our very own grand little love story, and so of course, we want to relive it.

Technically, we didn't do more than kiss that first year.

It was another year of online flirting and banter before we actually connected in person again at the convention. I'm a late bloomer, I guess, and a slow burn. I like being wooed. But Mel was patient and understanding and very, very charming. Right away, it was like we spoke the same language. We could talk about books and videogames and anime for hours. She was better with people than I was, less shy but still introverted, happily living on a small hobby farm in the country where she worked as an equine veterinarian. I lived many hours away in a bigger city, working mostly remotely in IT. At first, our physical distance made me reluctant to pursue things with her because why begin a relationship that has such a big obstacle in place from the very beginning? But if there was one thing that Mel was good at, it was making me believe. Believe in myself, and in her, and in the beauty of what we could have together. I'm grateful to her for that and for so much more.

Scanning the crowd for her face, I can't help but think back to our first time here. I mean, our first time being intimate. My first time ever.

I know it would strike most people as strange that we roleplayed even in our very first intimate encounter, but that's how we met, after all. Besides, sometimes pretending to be someone else can feel safer than being myself. Sometimes even more real, as I can explore parts of myself that don't see the light of day in my everyday life. I know I am so much braver when I am called by another name, when I feel myself in another's skin. In talking about why we chose our outfits that first year, I admitted that I fantasized about being with the Viking fighter. She was so fierce, so honorable, loyal, and brave. I admired those things. I liked her tattoos and her battle-ax and her scars. I found them somewhat intimidating, for sure, but sexy as hell. Eventually, after months of online flirting, Mel offered to make my fantasy come true, promising to dress up as this character at the next Comic Con, where we planned to meet up once more. That left me to play my part, but choosing was easy because in the game, the clan warrior seduces the sweet village huntress, taking her to her bed in the longhouse. This role was easy to play because it required me to be in awe, desirous, but uncertain, precisely how I already felt.

And our first encounter was just as exquisite as I could ever have hoped. Mel was…practiced and confident, which I truly appreciated given my complete lack of experience. Which I think she appreciated right back. Getting to be the teacher. The master. Being the only one ever to have known me this way. When she went down on me for the first time, I swear I believed in magic because I knew I was hers forevermore. That I would go to any length to keep her. To have more of this astonishing feeling in my life. I wanted to wrap myself up in her and tangle our lives together inextricably. Since I had always been such a fiercely independent lone wolf, we both like to think that that was quite the testament to her lovemaking skills. She teased me and pleasured me for hours on hours that weekend, and we barely left our hotel room as I learned to love her back. In fact, I don't think we went to a single workshop or Q and A that year.

I blush at the remembrance, and the word "becomingly" pops into my head. In historical fiction, women are always blushing "becomingly." Is Mel watching me now? Does she find me becoming? Can she guess what I'm thinking about? How I'm anticipating her hands upon me once more? How beneath my pannier and bloomers, I am already tingling at the thought of her mouth enticing me to release?

It's surprisingly difficult to spot her. You'd think that by now we'd be so familiar to each other that we'd spot each other right away. But every year, I'm left searching and searching. Admittedly, she has an advantage since she's more comfortable with crowds and will easily move within their midst while I tend to cling to the comfort of the outskirts of a throng. I think she knows this and makes me wait on purpose. Teasing me. Building up my longing. Watching me search for her.

She's also an incredible chameleon. She can truly transform her look, her gait, her very energy to embody someone else. It's shocking really. But then also exciting. In reality, she's the only woman I've ever slept with. And yet, in my imagination, it truly feels like I've slept with dozens and dozens of different characters. Roleplay is our thing. Our kink. Our unique bond and connection. We sew costumes and 3D print props. We create elaborate backstories and sets for our lovemaking. It's wild. More than I could ever have dreamed.

Eventually, I convinced my boss to allow me to work remotely so that we could move in together. At first, I was nervous about the labor demands of living on a hobby farm. But to be honest, I think her real hobby on the farm is fucking me silly in odd outdoor locations. Let's just say that I've been tied to many a tree and lost my virtue to a rakish bandit more than once.

In the videogame we both like, there's this one scene where the Viking fake-kidnaps a slutty queen to free her from her loveless marriage. The whole thing is staged to give both monarchs a chance to move on with their lives since divorce was difficult to attain. But as the Viking carries her away over her shoulder, like a stereotypical brute, the queen cries out with super poor acting, "Oh no, whatever will become of my honor now?" It's the cheesiest, fakest line, and it always cracks us up, so we use it mockingly a lot during our own encounters that include capture. "Unhand me, you beast." "You, sir, are no gentleman." All these ridiculous, melodramatic staples are such fun to throw around.

Generally speaking, Mel is more fluid in her gender expression than I am. She prefers to roleplay as a warrior or adventurer of some type. Often a cheeky rogue. I like being a witch. I have a couple of "goddess wands"—aka crystal dildos—that I like to charge under the full moon, then use on her by the pond. And some rose quartz yoni eggs that I like to make her wear as she goes about her day, just to remind her that she is loved and that her pussy is absolute fucking magic.

I also like being a princess. But a bitchy, difficult one. One who needs a firm hand.

So although it's a little on the girlie side for her, I was so excited about the idea of being Marie Antoinette that Mel graciously agreed to play the princess to my queen. How could she not when I enticed her with the image of eating me out under all my petticoats while I feasted on cake? The image amused both of us, and now, here we are. Or at least, here I am. She remains elusive for the moment.

I start to walk the perimeter of the room, scanning. I see plenty of anime girls, elves, superheroes, aliens, monsters. No doomed eighteenth-century royal personages, though. I fan myself and resign myself to waiting. Waiting can be fun, however, when it's filled with anticipatory thoughts of what's to come. Will she be able to breathe if she tries to go down on me under all the layers of this dress?

There's a famous portrait of the Princess de Lamballe painted by Duplessis. She's posing on an elegant couch, her left arm resting on a fancy pillow while her right hand rests in her lap, cupping a handful of delicate flowers. Her dress is lacy and blue-gray. She looks relaxed, happy, and slightly sly. Like she has a secret. Oh, and her right nipple is showing. Just barely peeking out over the trim of her bodice lace. The left is suggested by a shadow if you scrutinize closely. Which I have. I love this portrait. An antique homage to the nip slip. How delightfully naughty. Thinking of it, I wonder if I can convince Mel to let me take pictures of her posed similarly in our hotel room. For our own private collection, of course. When we die, someone needs to destroy a lot of risqué photos and toys before our executors show up to go through our things.

That portrait isn't even the most risqué of "la Princesse"

though. The French created all kinds of pornographic posters depicting her and Marie engaged in all sorts of imaginative erotic dalliances. We should recreate those too, I think. I can picture it. Pinching her nipples, laying the full weight of my naked body atop hers. Ideally lounging on a ludicrously expensive divan, but I'm sure the hotel sofa will do. Our imaginations and some candlelight should help. Mostly, the drawings are just Marie being finger-fucked by her lady friend against ornamental backdrops. I like the way her skirts billow about her as she lounges, indulging her perverse desires. Such shameless debauchery. I can't wait to feel Mel's hand first start its search for my most hidden spaces beneath all these layers and layers of fabric. Will she be bold? Sneaky? Sweet? Teasing? I never know how she'll approach as any given character, and that's half the fun.

And what about me? How will I approach her? Should I punish her for making me wait? She's *my* lady-in-waiting, after all. It's literally her job to service me. Please me. Indulge my every whim. And goodness knows that Marie was known for having whims. Will I feed her cake by hand? Lick icing off her famously immortalized right nipple? Will I order her to strip to her bloomers and then paddle her bottom for irritating me so? Will I loose her lacings in a frenzy or take things slowly, drawing out the pleasure of disrobing her?

One thing is for sure. I plan to take her up against the giant hotel window, the one overlooking the falls. Another sacrosanct tradition. The falls look so beautiful at night, all lit up in festive colors. And so powerful. Gushing and gushing ferociously like her orgasms each time, soaking my arm, my face, anything I'm wearing when I fuck her just so, just the way I know she likes after so many years of vigorous practice.

I can feel my pussy becoming wet at the thought and squirm. What's taking her so long? If she's watching, I'm sure she knows just what kind of unladylike thoughts I'm having. I'm blushing again, and I fan myself more forcefully, trying to calm myself, to appease the fever rising in me. But the images are flooding now. All the times we've fucked up against that window. All the outfits and interactions. The cheesy lines. The cries and moans. The ways I've taken her. All the ways she's taken me. *Fuck.* I start to sweat, and the corset feels uncomfortably restrictive of my breathing. I shift my weight and pull at my costume, starting to feel overwhelmed and breathless.

"Are you okay? Do you need help?"

The magic, fateful words spoken once again.

And all is right with my world once again.

Her eyes lock with mine, and she looks so different, so uncharacteristically feminine and yet still that same woman I have known and loved through so many time periods and costumes, that I start to laugh.

I still don't know why I do this.

But it doesn't matter. For she has taken my hand and is leading me away from the crowd. Away from the people and the noise and the busyness. She'll take me away to our own private wonderland, where we can be alone and as one together once again. We'll play. Dress up. Laugh. Love. Be silly together. Woo each other. Come over and over on each other's flesh. Over and over until the world is spinning and nothing makes sense except to hold on. To hold on to each other, and this weird and wonderful, extraordinary little thing we have created together.

We'll be together once more, rewriting our own epic romance against the majestic roaring backdrop of one of the great wonders of the world.

And then go back to our home, sweet home.

And start planning for next year.

About the Author

Raven Sky is a polyamorous queer femme who hails from Canada and is fueled by wanderlust, tea, books, and insatiable curiosity. She's a free-spirited dreamer who very much enjoys doing field research for her erotica. You can find more of her sexy stories in the Bold Strokes Books anthology *Escape to Pleasure: Lesbian Travel Erotica*.

Books Available From Bold Strokes Books

All That Remains by Sheri Lewis Wohl. Johnnie and Shantel might have to risk their lives—and their love—to stop a werewolf intent on killing. (978-1-63555-949-1)

Beginner's Bet by Fiona Riley. Phenom luxury Realtor Ellison Gamble has everything, except a family to share it with, so when a mix-up brings youthful Katie Crawford into her life, she bets the house on love. (978-1-63555-733-6)

Dangerous Without You by Lexus Grey. Throughout their senior year in high school, Aspen, Remington, Denna, and Raleigh face challenges in life and romance that they never expect. (978-1-63555-947-7)

Desiring More by Raven Sky. In this collection of steamy stories, a rich variety of lovers find themselves desiring more: more from a lover, more from themselves, and more from life. (978-1-63679-037-4)

Jordan's Kiss by Nanisi Barrett D'Arnuck. After losing everything in a fire, Jordan Phelps joins a small lounge band and meets pianist Morgan Sparks, who lights another blaze—this time in Jordan's heart. (978-1-63555-980-4)

Late City Summer by Jeanette Bears. Forced together for her wedding, Emily Stanton and Kate Alessi navigate their lingering passion for one another against the backdrop of New York City and World War II, and a summer romance they left behind. (978-1-63555-968-2)

Love and Lotus Blossoms by Anne Shade. On her path to self-acceptance and true passion, Janesse will risk everything—and possibly everyone—she loves. (978-1-63555-985-9)

Love in the Limelight by Ashley Moore. Marion Hargreaves, the finest actress of her generation, and Jessica Carmichael, the world's biggest pop star, rediscover each other twenty years after an ill-fated affair. (978-1-63679-051-0)

Two Winters by Lauren Emily Whalen. A modern YA retelling of Shakespeare's *The Winter's Tale* about birth, death, Catholic school, improv comedy, and the healing nature of time. (978-1-63679-019-0)

Suspecting Her by Mary P. Burns. Complications ensue when Erin O'Connor falls for top real estate saleswoman Catherine Williams while investigating racism in the real estate industry; the fallout could end their chance at happiness. (978-1-63555-960-6)

Calumet by Ali Vali. Jaxon Lavigne and Iris Long had a forbidden small-town romance that didn't last, and the consequences of that love will be uncovered fifteen years later at their high school reunion. (978-1-63555-900-2)

Her Countess to Cherish by Jane Walsh. London Society's material girl realizes there is more to life than diamonds when she falls in love with a non-binary bluestocking. (978-1-63555-902-6)

Hot Days, Heated Nights by Renee Roman. When Cole and Lee meet, instant attraction quickly flares into uncontrollable passion, but their connection might be short-lived as Lee's identity is tied to her life in the city. (978-1-63555-888-3)

Never Be the Same by MA Binfield. Casey meets Olivia, and sparks fly in this opposites attract romance that proves love can be found in the unlikeliest places. (978-1-63555-938-5)

Quiet Village by Eden Darry. Something not quite human is stalking Collie and her niece, and she'll be forced to work with undercover reporter Emily Lassiter if they want to get out of Hyam alive. (978-1-63555-898-2)

Shaken or Stirred by Georgia Beers. Bar owner Julia Martini and home health aide Savannah McNally attempt to weather the storms brought on by a mysterious blogger trashing the bar, family feuds they knew nothing about, and way too much advice from way too many relatives. (978-1-63555-928-6)

The Fiend in the Fog by Jess Faraday. Can four people on different trajectories work together to save the vulnerable residents of East London from the terrifying fiend in the fog before it's too late? (978-1-63555-514-1)

The Marriage Masquerade by Toni Logan. A no-strings-attached marriage scheme to inherit a Maui B&B uncovers unexpected attractions and a dark family secret. (978-1-63555-914-9)

BOLDSTROKESBOOKS.COM

Looking for your next great read?

Visit BOLDSTROKESBOOKS.COM
to browse our entire catalog of paperbacks, ebooks,
and audiobooks.

Want the first word on what's new?
Visit our website for event info,
author interviews, and blogs.

Subscribe to our free newsletter for sneak peeks,
new releases, plus first notice of promos
and daily bargains.

SIGN UP AT
BOLDSTROKESBOOKS.COM/signup

Bold Strokes Books
Quality and Diversity in LGBTQ Literature

*Bold Strokes Books is an award-winning publisher
committed to quality and diversity in LGBTQ fiction.*

www.ingramcontent.com/pod-product-compliance
Lightning Source LLC
Chambersburg PA
CBHW022015010726
47494CB00003B/1042